Hungarian Rhapsody

by
Wendy Teller

ISBN 978-1-7340758-1-6
Printed in the United States of America

Credits
Cover Design: Richard F. Weyand.
Cover Photo: Main Street, Nagykanizsa, Hungary, 1905
Postcard. Photographer unknown. Public domain.

- Pages 19, 84, 129, 250: King James Bible, public domain.
- Pages 33, 35, 259, 260: A holnap asszonayai (Women of Tomorrow) by Ede Harkanyi, public domain. Trans. by Wendy Teller, all rights reserved.
- Page 61: derived from a 17th cent. English Ballad. Public domain.
- Pages 185, 186: Fruits of Philosophy, by Charles Knowlton, MD. Public domain.
- Page 250: The Two Donkeys, by Christian Morgenstern, public domain. Translation by Max Knight used with permission.
- Page 252: The Snail's Monologue, by Christian Morgenstern, public domain. Translation by Max Knight used with permission.
- Page 253: The Snail's Soliloquy, by Christian Morgenstern, public domain. Translation by Howard Stern used with permission.
- Page 254-255: The Fisches Nachtgesang, by Christian Morgenstern, public domain. Translation by Max Knight used with permission.

Published by Weyand Associates, Inc.
Bloomington, Indiana, USA
December, 2019

www.weyandassociates.com

Also by Wendy Teller
Becoming Mia

This book is dedicated to Ede Harkányi, who
devoted his life to the rights of women.

Contents

June 1905, Nagykanizsa, the Austro-Hungarian Empire

The sun had barely risen over the horizon as three peasant women carried baskets on their covered heads, baskets heavy with early summer fruits: cherries, raspberries and apricots. Their stout figures, enlarged by their broad skirts and black shawls, walked north and east, to Nagykanizsa. On market days the path was filled with such women, their leather boots kicking up the road's dust. But today was not market. Today two rich Nagykanizsa families would be joined in matrimony and only the finest fruits, the most perfect flowers were good enough for the occasion.

A flower-filled cart, which had started out before the peasant women, stood in front of the Church of the Sacred Heart, where the aunt of the bride directed the parish women in the decoration of the chapel. Father Joseph, who would preside over the wedding, stood aside, scowling, impatient with the intruders.

Once the roses, the daisies, and the baby breath had been properly placed, the half empty cart traveled several blocks to the City Club, where the wedding dinner and reception would be held. There the remainder of the cart's cargo joined the fruit brought by the peasant women.

Having delivered their goods, the peasants retraced their dusty path to their thatch-covered homes, leaving the cobbled streets free for the citizens who would attend the wedding, the bankers, the factory owners, the merchants – the important men who made Nagykanizsa the business center of Zala County. Of course Count Batthyány would not attend – he was an aristocrat who did not mingle with businessmen – but there had been rumors that the father of the groom, the late Mr. Herczeg, might have been ennobled. He had constructed many important public buildings: the railway station in Piski, the church in Kaposvár, the courthouse in Subotica, and more. The emperor himself had visited the construction site of the barracks in Csáktornya.

Those who would attend the wedding, the families of the well-to-do, were getting ready, the ladies putting on their best dresses and fixing their hair in fine dos, the gentlemen wearing their Sunday suits, combing their beards, and waxing their mustaches.

Mr. Weisel, owner of the iron factory and the machine works, inspected himself in the mirror: his plump face; his hair, still dark, but receding; his trimmed beard on his heavy jowls. He was a substantial man, in stature and in his community. He had hoped his daughter would be the bride today, but the groom was ready to marry and his daughter was still too young. Mr. Weisel sighed. There would be other fine men for his Ella to marry.

Wedding Preparations

Ella was not getting dressed.

She stood against the wall, her fingers at her back running up and down the laces, searching for a bow.

The red in Mother's face highlighted the dark mole on her chin. "Turn around this instant!"

Ella shook her head.

"Miss, it just needs to be a little tighter." Therese held up her hand, her fingers indicating a tiny space.

The bone stays cut into Ella's ribs with each trickle of air she sucked in. She found a knot rather than a bow. Her fingers worked to loosen it. She exhaled, slackening the laces. Her fingers rolled the ties back and forth, finding a loop. Sliding her forefinger between the laces, she pulled the knot open and, running her hands up the corset back, she loosened the ties. She inhaled deeply, ignoring the oppressive sweetness of Mother's perfume.

"You impudent girl. Turn around and let Therese do her job." Mother's lips pursed. "You will make us all late!"

Ella shook her head. She took another deep breath, fully expanding her rib cage and filling her lungs with air, glorious air.

Ella's little sister Clara, dressed in her party clothes, tugged at her mother's sleeve. "Mama?"

"Clara, what are you doing?" Mother's stormy face looked down at her other daughter. "Oh, never mind. Go get your father!"

Ella looked after Clara with envy as she ran out the door. She was still young. She was allowed to wear loose clothing. How Ella longed for those more comfortable days.

Ella's hair, swept up in a complicated style, felt like it was being pulled out, centimeter by centimeter. Why did being properly dressed amount to torture? She released an auburn lock and twirled it, feeling her shoulders relax as the silky strand slid across her finger tips.

"Ella! Stop!" Clara gone, Mother's glare returned to Ella. "You are ruining your hair and Therese worked so hard to make you look pretty!"

Ella dropped her hand by her side and stared at her mother. Would she be like her mother twenty years from now, angry and sputtering? Ella promised herself that would not happen.

"What is going on?" Father stood at the door, his walking stick in his hand, his tie just so. "This should be a good day, a holiday, a festival day. So what's the fuss?"

"Deal with your daughter." Mother spat the words at her husband. "She won't let Therese dress her."

"Why not?" Father's eyes glimmered merrily. He was ready for the ceremony and, more important, the party ahead.

"Ella, my princess, why won't you get dressed?"

Ella sighed and then took another deep breath.

"My dress doesn't fit."

Father tucked his chin and frowned.

"Doesn't fit?"

"Of course it fits!" Mother sharp voice cut through the moment of peace between father and daughter." She just won't let Therese tighten her corset, so the dress can be buttoned."

Father glared at his wife, then turned his attention back to his daughter.

"Ella, my dear, be a good girl. Put on your clothes, so we can go to the wedding."

"Father, I can't breathe when the corset is tightened."

"Don't you want to look pretty?"

As Father approached her, Ella inhaled his scent of tobacco and mint.

He tucked the loosened strand of Ella's hair behind her ear.

"You're eighteen and beautiful. The most beautiful girl in Nagykanizsa. Maybe the most beautiful in all of Hungary."

He lifted her chin.

"It's time to look for a husband for you and you want to find a good rich fellow. You need to look pretty."

Mother's voice rose from behind Father. "The sooner we get her married, the better."

Ella locked her gaze on Father. "The dress is too small."

He shrugged. "Then wear another dress."

Mother snorted. "You think we have another party dress for Ella?" She shook her head. "I certainly don't have enough money for an extra dress for her."

Father scowled at his wife. "Mrs. Weisel, enough."

He turned his attention back to his daughter. "Ella, you may come to the wedding if you get dressed. If you don't want to get dressed, you will have to stay at home."

He turned and walked out of the room, the tap of his walking stick punctuating every other step.

Mother looked at the empty doorway, nodding. "All right. Ella, we have no time to waste. Let Therese fit your corset properly."

Her eyes fixed on her mother, Ella shook her head. She would not wear that thing. She didn't want to sit through the wedding mass anyhow.

"Very well. Ella, you are to stay in this room while we are away. No dinner. No books. A good chance for you to catch up on your mending and needle work."

Mother turned to Therese. "And you are to stay with her." Mother nodded her head as she formulated her plan." To make sure she does as she is told."

Ella knew Mother was punishing Therese too, to make the hours ahead even more unpleasant for both unhappy women, forced to miss a party, each resenting the other. And compliant Therese would forgo food if Mother commanded it.

"Mother, can't at least Therese have something to eat?"

Therese glanced at Ella.

Mother's lips smiled, but her eyes were stony. "Oh, I suppose she can find something in the kitchen." Mother turned toward Therese. "Cook has banked the fire, so nothing warm, but I am sure you can find something there."

Mother's skirts swished as she left, pulling the door closed behind her.

"Help me out of this thing!" Ella couldn't wait to get into her skirt and blouse, back to her real self, not the doll Mother and Father planned to marry off.

"Yes, Miss." Therese did as she was asked.

Oh, Ella thought, does this woman – for she was a good ten years older than Ella – does she have no backbone? Why does she not rage against the injustice? It was not Therese's fault the dress was so small.

Therese was a nuisance, this companion Mother thought so necessary. No, she was not a companion. She was a guard, a prison guard, to make sure that Ella did not misbehave. It didn't matter that all eligible young women had "companions". Her friend Zsuzsi had one too. But Zsuzsi was the perfect young lady, so she got along with her minder.

Ella threw the corset on the floor, gratefully buttoned up her bodice, and slipped on her blouse and skirt. She loosened her hair, placing the pins in a box at her dressing table. Massaging her scalp, she sat on her bed, looking around the room she shared with Therese, her prison for the next several hours. So pretty, with its pale green walls, translucent white curtains, and white brocade bedspreads. So perfect with the cherry wood inlaid with oak in the bed's headboard, the wash table, the chairs, in every piece of furniture in the room down to the frame on the mirror. So prettily, perfectly awful.

The sound of raised voices penetrated the door.

"Mother, it is simply not fair!"

"Well, you don't have to keep my unruly daughter under control, so you might think it unfair, but that's too bad."

"But Therese has done nothing wrong!"

Ella had to smile. She rarely agreed with her brother, Miklos, but today he was making perfect sense.

"Just because Ella is impossible, why should Therese suffer?"

"Because she is paid to suffer!"

Therese moved closer to the door, her ear nearly touching it.

Miklos's words grew louder. "Mother, that is not very Christian!"

Miklos had as impudent a tongue as Ella's, but her mother tolerated him. Because he was six years older? Maybe. Because he was male? Probably. Mother always wilted in front of men.

Miklos's voice took a sweeter tone. "Besides, Clara will be happier if Therese comes. Therese always entertains her."

"Miklos, we don't have time for this. We are going to be late as it is." Mother's sigh was audible through the door. "Maybe you're right. Therese can come. But tell Ella, she is to stay in her room. No dinner."

The door burst open, framing a grinning Miklos. "Therese, put on your good dress. You're coming to the party!"

He smiled as he turned to his sister. "But no party for you.

And no dinner."

Ella returned his smile. "Who wants to sit through another mass? We have to do that once a week anyhow."

"No doubt the mass will be splendid, not a prayer or a hymn left out. But the party! It will be exquisite! Endre Herczeg loves to show off his...." Miklos rubbed his thumb against his first two fingers. "You can bet there will be the best food, and wine, and I hear Csárdás dancers will come. And there will be a Viennese orchestra, so we shall waltz!"

He twirled in place, his arms around an imaginary partner. He looked back at his sister, his lips twisted in a smirk. "Too bad for you, but you'll have a great time with your needle work."

Ella's smile remained. "Eat yourself sick. Drink yourself dumb."

Miklos snickered."And, of course, you won't get to see your friend Ede."

He understood his weapons, leaving the most lethal until last.

Ella turned her gaze to the window, so her brother couldn't see her face.

Fire!

After the bustle of the family's wedding preparations, the house was still. Ella had never been in the house totally alone before. No Mother, Father, Clara, or Miklos, no nanny or tutor or companion, not even Cook or Maid were at home. It felt strange and she wandered from room to room, without purpose. She stopped in Clara's room, which once had been the nursery. There, all these years later, was the charred spot, where a cinder from the fire had scarred the floor.

On that day so long ago, Mother had said Ella and Zsuzsi were too young to be with the adults in the salon, so they were confined to the nursery. Mother was having her afternoon, attended by everyone in Nagykanizsa. At least that was what Mother said. But that was clearly wrong since Ella was excluded.

It would have been better to be in the salon. Ella's brother Miklos was there, and their friend Ede was there too. They were ten, which Mother considered old enough. She and Zsuzsi were only four. Ella thought four was old enough to attend Mother's afternoon.

Ella nibbled a poppy seed roll and let the honey and nut mixture sit on her tongue, savoring the sweetness. But she was sure they had even better things to eat and drink in the salon. And she'd rather be with the boys.

Nanny was helping Zsuzsi learn to spool knit, a way to make a long cord. Nanny had tried to interest Ella in spool knitting too, letting her choose any color yarn from the basket.

But Ella was more interested in the pencil and paper Father had given her. She had begged for them. Father seemed uncertain until she said she wanted to draw designs like the ones on the iron railings made in his factory.

She sat at the table grasping the cylindrical pencil, but it always seemed to squirm from her fingers. She drew lines. Horizontal lines, vertical lines, slanted lines. She drew circles. Circles with a tail going down one side or the other, like the cat sitting on a fence at Grandmother's farm. She drew circles with the tail going up, like the cat when the dog barked at her. Ella leaned back in the wooden chair, pulled a strand of hair from her clip, and rolled it with her fingers. She scanned the paper with the marks she had drawn. Miklos and Ede drew such things. They called it writing. She wanted to write too.

"Are you girls having fun?" Ella looked up to see Zsuzsi's mother at the nursery door, carrying her daughter's coat.

"Oh, yes, Mutti!" Zsuzsi jumped up carrying the spool, the cord, and the yarn. "See what Nanny taught me!"

"Very nice dear." She patted her daughter on the head. "But it's time to go home."

Zsuzsi's lower lip protruded as she shook her head side to side. "I don't want to go!"

Ella was surprised. Zsuzsi never complained.

Nanny stood. "You may take the spool and yarn with you." She smoothed her dress. "You can return the spool when you have finished your cord."

Zsuzsi turned to Nanny, her eyes wide. "May I?"

Nanny chuckled. "Of course."

Mutti nodded at Nanny. "How kind of you!" She looked at her daughter. "Say thank you to Nanny."

Zsuzsi muttered a distracted thank you as she stuffed the cord, spool, and yarn into the little blue bag Nanny had given her.

When they had gone, Ella ran down the hall to Miklos' room. The boys sat on the floor and were lazily tossing a red ball back and forth. She followed the ball with her eyes. She wanted to hold it, feel its surface. She stepped between the boys.

"Let me have the ball!"

Miklos threw the ball high in the air, so that Ella couldn't reach it.

Ede caught it and both boys laughed.

Ella fought to hold back her tears. Ede gently tossed the ball to Ella. She caught it. Surprised at how easily she'd won the ball, she rubbed both her hands over its surface.

Miklos stood. "Give me that ball!"

Ella backed away from her brother hiding the ball behind her back. Miklos hadn't shared it with her, so she wasn't going to share it with him. He stepped toward her so she threw the ball to Ede, who tossed it back to Ella. Miklos glared at his friend then, his arm outstretched, tried to grab the ball.

Ella ran to the nursery, both boys following her. She turned when she was in her room and looked for Ede, but Miklos stood between them. His hand was out, reaching for the ball.

She threw the ball as hard as she could over Miklos' head. Miklos grabbed her hand just as she released it. She followed the ball's path with her eyes. Over Miklos. Over Ede. Against the corner of the room. Off the wall next to the bed. Against the oil lamp, which teetered and fell on the bed. A lick of yellow escaped. Smoke. Red. Yellow. A putrid smell, like the outhouse at Grandmother's farm.

Nanny dumped blankets on the flaming bed.

"What is going on here?" Mother's full figure filled the door, her fists on her hips.

"We've had an accident, ma'am."

Mother ran in, her hand fanning the smoke. "How on earth?"

Thinking back to that day, Ella laughed. How Mother fumed! And she remembered Father's alarmed voice from the hall.

"What's the smoke?"

Mother stepped back to let Father in.

"And the smell!" He coughed and sputtered. "Who did this?"

Nanny's face whitened. "The children came running in. Next thing I knew the oil lamp was on the bed." Her face, usually so cheerful, was drawn. "I had just lit it...."

Mother stepped forward. "Keep the children under control!"

Father glowered at Mother. "Enough, Mrs. Weisel!"

"The lamp set the featherbed on fire." Nanny looked down. "I... I threw all the blankets I could find on it." She glanced at the untidy heap, a bit of black peaked out from the pile of white embroidered blankets.

"You've done well Nanny!" Father smiled and patted her on the shoulder. "Without you the building might have burned down!"

He turned and scowled at the children. "Now, who would like to explain?"

"It was Miklos!" Ella's voice was loud and raspy. She had to get her words in before the boys did. "He threw the ball, and it hit the lamp."

Miklos stood tall, his lips tight, his hands balled in fists. "I did not." His chin jutted out. "It was Ella. She threw the ball."

"No." Ede's voice was calm. "I did it. I threw the ball." He shrugged, a quick smile flickering on his lips.

Ella stared. Why would Ede claim to be the guilty one?

Father chuckled. "Hmmm. I see. Three children. Three stories."

He stroked his chin and looked at Nanny. "Do you know

what happened?"

"I was busy straightening up, sir. The children ran in, and the fire started."

Father nodded and turned back to the children. "Who is going to confess?"

Miklos shook his head. "Ede already confessed, Father."

Father's glare focused on Miklos. "So Ede did it?"

Miklos looked down and shook his head. "No. It was Ella."

Father eyes settled on Ella. "And you say...."

Ella stared back. She could not let Ede take the blame. She wanted Miklos to take the blame. "It was Miklos' fault. He knocked my hand...."

"See." Miklos shouted. "Ella did throw the ball."

Father nodded. "I see." Compressing his lips he nodded again. "You're all guilty."

Miklos blurted out, "What?"

"Yes. You are guilty, Miklos, for not playing nicely with your sister."

Miklos looked down.

"Ella, you not only threw the ball, but you knocked over the lamp."

Ella returned Father's stern stare, not blinking, not flinching.

"And, Ella, you lied."

Ella did not look down.

"Lying is a sin, Ella. Do not lie."

Ella wrinkled her nose, still staring at her father. She would not dare do this to Mother.

Father turned to Ede. "You lied too, Ede."

Ede looked down. "Yes, Uncle."

"Why did you lie?"

"Because, sir,...." Ede looked up at Father. "I thought it was a gentleman's duty to protect his lady."

Father chuckled.

Ella stared at Ede and stamped her foot. "I don't need to be protected." She clenched her fists. "I am not a lady. I am a girl." She pounded her feet on the floor. "And girls are just as good as boys."

Ella stomped her foot again, remembering that day, when she first realized Ede was her friend.

Learning to Read

Ede was her friend, even then, when she was only four and he was ten. Thinking of it now, it seemed incredible that he would spend time with a child so much younger than he, and a girl at that. But her four-year-old self realized he was the one who could help her get the things she wanted, and the first thing she wanted was to learn to read.

Ede and Miklos attended the Piarist boys' school. The day after the fire, when the boys had returned from school, Ella went into Miklos' room. Ede lay on the bed, reading a book, and Miklos sat at the table, pen in hand, drawing.

"Ede, I want to show you something."

He looked up. "What?"

"I can't tell you. I have to show you."

He closed his book and followed Ella down the hall. She walked past the nursery, down the stairs, and into the salon.

"This mysterious object, it's not in the nursery?"

Ella wrinkled her nose. "It could be, but the nursery still smells like bad eggs."

She hadn't noticed the stink when she woke, but after breakfast, when she had gone back to her room, the smell of burnt wool, cotton, and feathers overwhelmed her. She had pleaded with Nanny to go outside, and they managed to stay away most of the day.

Ella didn't want to sleep there tonight, but Mother had said she had to, that Maid had aired the room and all the burnt linens had been removed. When Ella still complained, Mother said she had to suffer the consequences of her actions. It was, after all, her fault the room smelt, and she could consider this as she lay in bed. Ella knew any further complaints would lead to punishment, so she said no more.

Ella picked up a book and her pencil and paper, which lay on the table next to the sofa.

Ede pointed to the book.

"Where did you get that?"

"From Father's study."

Ede's brows lifted. "Does Uncle know you took one of his books?"

Ella shook her head.

"Well, maybe you should put it back, before he comes home."

Ella shook her head again.

"He might be angry you took it."

"I don't care." She compressed her lips and furrowed her brows. "I need to learn how to read and write, like you and Miklos."

"How are you planning to do that?"

"With Father's book."

She sat on the sofa and opened the book, looking at a page. She stared up at Ede.

"And you're going to help me."

"OK."

Ede turned the book around and replaced it in Ella hands. "This is the proper way up."

She ran her fingers across the page.

He scratched his head. "Why don't we use one of my books and put Uncle's book back, so he won't get mad?"

"OK."

Ede replaced the book on the shelf in Father's study and

retrieved one of his own from Miklos' room.

Looking back on it, Ella wondered whether Father would really have been upset. She hadn't considered it, but, of course, Ede would. That was Ede, always thinking about how other people would react, even when he was only ten.

That day, so long ago, they settled on the sofa, the book on Ella's lap, Ede so close to her she could smell the scent of fresh pine, the smell of his father's lumber yard. He pointed to a letter on the page.

"Here's an 'a'. That's a little 'a'. There is a big 'A'."

Ella ran her finger across the page.

"There's another 'a'. And another." She looked up at him.

"Yes!"

He nodded and took up the pencil and paper.

"You draw a little 'a' like this." He wrote an 'a' on the paper and showed it to her. "Can you write one?"

She took the paper and, biting her lower lip and gripping the pencil, copied Ede's 'a.' She looked at him.

"That's great!"

He took the paper and drew again. "Here's a big 'A.' Can you write a big 'A?'"

She took the paper and drew. She looked at him.

"What are you two doing here?"

They looked up into Mother's scowling face.

Ella grimaced. "The nursery stinks."

"And whose fault is that?"

Mother's skirts swished as she entered the room.

"I don't want you here, dirtying the salon. It's for company. Next thing you know you'll start a fire here!"

"Auntie, we are being very careful." It was true. They hadn't disturbed a thing.

"I should hope!"

Mother looked down on the children.

"In any case, Ede needs to go home for tea. Ede's father and brother are back from their travels, and he needs to see them."

"No!" Ella kicked her legs as she yelled. "He is teaching me to read, and he is staying here 'til I learn."

Ede hugged her. "Ella, you've already learned all about 'a.'"

"No. We just got started!"

"It's OK, Ella. You practice your 'a's. Tomorrow we will work on 'b'."

Kis Maria

Thinking about that day, when she began to learn to read, Ella wandered down the hall, past Miklos' room and her own. She took the stairs to the main floor of the apartment, walked across the hall into the salon. Three large windows looked out on Fő út, Main Street. A sofa, stuffed and buttoned, sat against the wall opposite the windows, with two matching chairs facing it. Above the sofa was a painting done some years ago of Clara, Miklos, and herself. She had never liked that painting.

But she loved the sofa, where she and Ede had spent many hours, a book on her lap, her finger tracing the words, he helping when she stumbled. He had taught her to read Hungarian and German and Latin too. He said teaching her Latin helped him remember his lessons. Then, when Clara was born and Alexa came to be Ella's tutor, Alexa taught both of them English.

She thought of the day she and Ede were reading the Bible, a way to study for her catechism class. She remembered reading the unforgettable sentence:

How can this be, since I know not man?

Ella didn't understand. "The Virgin Mary didn't know any men? She didn't know her father?" Ella looked at Ede, hoping for an explanation.

Ede's brows furrowed as he looked past Ella.

Thinking back to that day, Ede's willingness to explain

astounded Ella. She wondered whether he realized he was telling her forbidden secrets. Probably he didn't.

That day, Ede looked past her and then refocused on her.

"I do understand." He sighed. "But it's going to take a little explaining...."

"Yes." Ella's fingers rolled a strand of her hair. "I'm listening."

"OK." He smiled at her. "Remember when Zsarátnok had her foal?"

"Of course."

Zsarátnok, the chestnut mare, her favorite horse, had a beautiful black colt just before they had to come home from Grandmother's that summer.

"And remember when Ferenc put Lovag in the corral with Zsarátnok last summer."

Ella nodded.

"Remember what Lovag did?"

Ella pursed her lips, remembering the scene.

"Lovag was planting a seed in Zsarátnok."

Ella squinted. "What?"

"Just like Grandmother plants her tomato seeds at Easter, to grow tomato plants."

Ella's brows knitted.

"How did Lovag do that?"

"When he put his penis in Zsarátnok, he planted his seed."

Ella stared.

"And that seed grew into little Tábornok."

Ella loved Tábornok with his long wobbly legs, his wispy tail and his blue black coat. "Yuck." How could Tábornok be the result of Lovag's penis?

"I know." Ede nodded. "It is yucky." He held her eyes. "But it is true."

Ella hugged herself and her body shook. "Yuck. Yuck. Yuck."

Ede sighed. "Yes. But that is how a baby horse is made." He bit his lower lip. "And that is how a baby person is made too."

"No!" Ella fisted her hands and shook her head.

Ede nodded not letting her deny this truth. "That's how Clara was made."

Ella closed her eyes, imagining her parents....

"That was how you were made."

She willed the image of Mother and Father out of her mind.

"And that was how I was made too."

Ella opened her eyes. She wanted not to think of these things. Better to think of her catechism.

"What does this have to do with Mary not knowing any man, not even her father?"

"When Mary says she doesn't know any men, she means that she has never...." Ede looked past Ella and then turned his gaze to her again. "It means that no man had done that to her."

"Oh."

"That the holy spirit planted a seed in her without...." Ede cleared his throat. "Well, Jesus was planted without that happening and that's why Mary is called 'virgin'."

"Oh." Ella felt comforted. "So I could have a baby without...."

Ede chuckled. "I don't know...."

"Well, if Mary could, why can't I?"

"Well...." Ede's rich laugh filled the room. "God loved Mary very much. She was special."

"Maybe, if I were called Mary, God would love me just as much and then...."

"I'm not sure that would be enough."

"Maybe not enough, but it would at least be a start."

Ella pushed the book to the side, stood and faced Ede, her hands on her hips. "Call me Mary."

"Yes, Little Mary." He ruffled her hair. "Yes, Kis Maria!"

Ella sat on the sofa, smiling as she remembered her nickname, Kis Maria. Only Ede called her Kis Maria.

But her smile faded, when she thought of Mother. Mother had had a different reaction to her plan.

Virgin Mary

She remembered Mother standing at the door to her room, hands on hips, a frown twisting her face. The look was similar to the look she had had this morning, when Therese tried to tighten the corset. Mother's shrill voice was impatient.

"Ella, are you ready to go to your catechism class?"

Ella sat at the table reading the Bible.

"Ella!" Mother's voice pierced the quiet of the room. "Answer me!"

Ella slowly lifted her head and looked at Mother. "There is no Ella here. I'm Mary. I'm Virgin Mary!"

Mother pushed Ella out of her chair. "What nonsense is this?"

"I'm not Ella. Call me Virgin Mary."

"I have no time for this." She shoved Ella out of the room and toward the stairs. "Get your coat on. You'll be late for Father Joseph. You don't want to be late!"

Ella descended the stairs several steps ahead of Mother's hand.

"I don't need to go to catechism class. I call myself Virgin Mary. God will love me and I don't need catechism or Father Joseph or any of that, because I call myself Virgin Mary and God loves me."

Mother grabbed her shoulder and twirled her around. "What nonsense is this?"

"I read it in the Bible. God loved Virgin Mary so he gave her Jesus and she didn't need to know any man." Ella smiled at her mother hoping she would understand. "So if I call myself Virgin Mary, God will love me and let me have a baby, like Clara, without knowing a man."

Mother's swift slap stung Ella's cheek.

Ella held her hands at her side, not giving Mother the satisfaction of seeing her touch her tingling cheek. "It's in the Bible."

She pulled on her coat and looked back at Mother. "And it's in the catechism too." She smiled at Mother, thinking she must know what was in the catechism.

"It says that Mary never knew a man." She buttoned her coat. "That means a man never put his penis in her."

Mother's second slap stung more than the first, but Ella balled her hands, letting her finger nails dig into her palms. Her cheek throbbed.

"Who told you that?"

Ella stared at her Mother blinking away the tears brimming in her eyes. "Ede explained all of it to me."

Mother's hand shook as she raised it for a third strike, but she looked toward the heavens instead. "Oh, Gabriella!"

Ella knew Mother meant Ede's dead mother, the woman Ella was named after.

"Gabriella, I promised you I would look after your son." She exhaled, shaking her head. "But this!"

They walked along Fő út in silence.

Ella decided it was best to keep her name-change plans to herself given Mother's reaction. Zsuzsi had told her Father Joseph would use a cane on what she called "sinners." That was another reason to keep her name change secret. Ella knew her lessons and replied to Father's questions when asked but otherwise sat quietly.

Miklos was waiting for her outside the church after class.

"Well, hello, Virgin Mary."

A sneer was smeared across his lips. "You did it this time!"

Ella started walking toward home, not wanting to talk to Miklos.

"You should have heard Mother shouting at Father!"

Ella walked ahead of him, but her ears strained to hear every word he said.

"Ede shall never set foot in this house again!"

Ella stopped and turned to her brother.

"That's what Mother said." Miklos grinned at her. "You really did it to Ede!"

Ella's throat tightened. She gulped.

"Nice work, Ella."

Ella raced home, tears streaming down her face.

Mother, waiting at the door, pushed her into her room.

"I suggest you get down on your knees, Ella, and pray to God to forgive your unclean... your blasphemous thoughts." She slammed the door closed as she left.

Ella lay down on the bed. She didn't care about Mother. Mother and her slaps. And she didn't care about Miklos. Miklos loved it when she was in trouble. But Ede. If Mother never let Ede come again. She hugged her knees to her chest and allowed herself to cry. Ede had done nothing wrong. He had only told her the truth. She was sure it was the truth. Why should Mother hate him, ban him for telling the truth? She turned towards the wall, staring at the pale green. She hated Mother.

She hated Mother all those years ago. And she hated her now. As she thought of it, she could not remember a time when she did not hate her mother. She wondered why her mother became a mother, because she didn't seem to like her children. Well, she liked Miklos, and maybe even Clara, but she certainly did not like Ella.

Ella sighed, thinking back to her younger self, sobbing on her bed. She remembered how the door had creaked open, and how she had heard Father's familiar tread. Step. Tap. Step. Tap. Father and his walking stick.

Would he use his walking stick like Father Joseph used his cane?

She felt Father's hand stroking her head. "There, there, little one." His low voice was mellow.

She turned to look at his whiskered face.

His lips turned up in a little smile. "I understand you have been informed about the forbidden fruit."

She nodded.

"I find your proposed solution to the problem of original sin ingenious." His smile grew as he shook his head. "But I don't think it will work."

He sat next to her on the bed. "And your mother is correct. It is blasphemous."

"Why would God be angry at me for trying to be good?"

He laughed. "Indeed." He pulled her up and enveloped her in his arms, rocking her. "I don't know how to answer that. I do not claim to understand God."

He held her at arm's length holding her gaze. "But I am quite sure that Mother and Father Joseph and everybody else in Nagykanizsa will think it is blasphemous. So I wouldn't talk about it anymore."

He studied her face. "Agreed?"

She nodded.

"But what about Ede?"

"Ah, yes, your friend Ede."

Ella inhaled sharply. This did not sound good. Father blamed Ede too.

"He just told me the truth!"

"Yes, yes." Father nodded. "But sometimes the truth should not be told." He pulled her to him. "Not to young girls."

She pushed him away. "You told me that I shouldn't lie."

He nodded and stroked his chin. "Yes, I did. You shouldn't lie."

"All I did was tell the truth. I didn't lie."

"Ah, yes. I see your point. But you shouldn't ram the truth down people's throats." He smiled and tilted his head. "Especially when they don't want to know the truth."

She shook her head in confusion. "How do you know when someone doesn't want to know the truth?"

Father's kind laugh comforted Ella. "My dear child, you ask all the unanswerable questions."

"But I want to know the truth. I always want to know the truth."

He nodded, put his hand in his vest pocket, and pulled out a mint candy.

"Well, then today has been a valuable lesson for you."

He unwrapped the candy and offered it to her.

"If you insist on knowing the truth, then at least be careful who you share it with."

She took the candy and felt tears welling in her eyes again, tears of gratitude for her father's kindness.

"But what about Ede? Miklos says Mother will never allow him to come here again."

"Never mind, little one. We will change her mind. Your friend Ede is a fine young man and he will always be welcome in my house."

Father had kept his promise. Ede continued to be a member of the family, just as he had been before the Kis Maria incident.

Ede Confesses

The Kis Maria incident had been so long ago. There had been many fights with Mother, but that had been the worst. After that battle perhaps both mother and daughter backed off. Ella sighed. Her stomach rumbled. She was hungry.

After gathering things from her room, she went to the kitchen to find something to eat. She set her books on the work table, next to the bread board, the honey pot, and the jug of milk. It seemed like sacrilege to put Dickens and Twain next to crumbs and sticky sweetness. But Ella needed company. She didn't usually eat alone.

Oh, what she would do to be sharing this meal, this milk and honey, with Ede!

She wrapped the shawl Ede had given her around her shoulders and ran her fingers across the embroidered flowers. It was a poor substitute for Ede, but it reminded her of him, with the faint scent of pine. She used to think Ede picked up this fragrance by playing in his father's lumber yard, but he didn't play there anymore. Even now, when he was with her, she could detect a whiff of evergreen.

She inhaled the fresh pine scent and thought of the times they would sit side by side, reading, studying, discussing new ideas. Those discussions, sometimes battles of wits, continued until Mother called them to a meal or sent Ede home.

Time with Ede seemed like a luxury now. He'd been away for what felt like forever. Six long years. He came home for Christmas and the summer, but those interludes were never long enough. At last his schooling was complete, so he would come home and she would be able to be with him again.

But not today. And if she could not share her food with her live friend, then she would share it with her book friends, her treasures that she had read with Ede when he was home. Besides, it gave her satisfaction. She was breaking her mother's commands. She was reading. Forbidden. And eating. Forbidden. Would her mother even notice? Maybe not. Or maybe she would and threaten God only knows what. That would be better, another chance to do battle.

Ella placed a few stained napkins, used for cleaning, in case there was a food disaster next to her friends. Huck Finn might get his feet muddy in the Mississippi, but she was determined he would not get them milky in Nagykanizsa.

She opened Twain's book, much less formal than the leather-bound copy of *The Tale of Two Cities*. The Dickens book had been a present from Ede, so it was precious, but *Huckleberry Finn* had been given to her by Mark Twain. It even had a dedication to her signed by the famous author. Besides, she understood Huck better than any of the characters in *The Tale*. Even though he was a peasant boy, the son of a drunk, she understood Huck's need to escape.

Reading Mark Twain used to be heavy going for Ella, but that was part of the fun. She remembered how Alexa had pronounced all those dialects, so different from the English in Dickens' book.

Ella missed Alexa, her companion before Therese. Sweet plump Alexa, always smiling, dimples in her round cheeks. But Alexa had gone home to Chicago to marry her childhood sweetheart and now Ella was stuck with Therese. She sighed and looked down at her books.

Ella loved Twain's note at the beginning of the story,

claiming he had used different dialects in the book. She tried to reproduce how the characters might sound, reading out loud.

Thump!

Ella jumped. Someone was pounding on the door to the servants' stairs. Who could it be? Everyone was either at the wedding or had the day off. Might it be a gypsy who had heard of the wedding, come into town to rob the houses while everyone was away? No. A gypsy, knowing the way of locks, would just come in silently and stealthily.

Thump! Thump!

She went to the door, and slowly cracked it open.

Ede! There was Ede, the one person she wanted to see.

But he was not right. He was dressed in his formal clothes, as he should be, since he was attending his brother's wedding. But his dark hair, usually so well-groomed was mussed, his collar tilted to one side, his usually calm eyes alert, scanning her face then searching the room.

"Ella! Thank God! I thought you might not be able to hear me."

His eyes settled on her, his beautiful eyes, today a pure green melding to golden brown at the center.

"Clara said you were confined to your room, but I didn't want to try to signal you from the street. People might see me. And I'm supposed to be at the wedding. I was so unhappy you were not there. Clara told me all about the argument...."

Ella swung the door wide and stood aside, waving him into the room.

"Come join my feast of milk and honey!"

She inhaled a breath of happiness. Ede, sweet Ede, was here. How she had longed for him and now he was here.

"I can stay but a moment. I don't want them to miss me at the party."

"But there will be so many people, surely one fewer won't make a difference."

"Oh, Ella, I needed to see you!"

"And I wanted to see you, the only reason I wanted to go."

"It's more than that. I need to talk to you."

Ella held her tongue. She wanted to tell Ede about the scene this morning, how impossible Mother was, and how she knew French as well as Therese, even if she couldn't speak as fast as Therese could. But she held her tongue because Ede's face was dark, his eyes solemn. Were his lips trembling?

"In case I can't finish what I have to say, in case we are interrupted, here is an essay. I want you to read it, so you might understand what I have to tell you a little better."

He pulled several pages from his vest pocket and handed them to her.

Ella set the papers on the table, all the time staring at this agitated character. This was not the usual Ede she had known all her life.

"What's wrong?"

His eyes settled on her, serious, maybe even hard.

"I've been with a woman."

He swept his hand across his forehead, patting down the locks that were out of place.

"A professional woman."

"A woman?" Ella shook her head, studying his face, his brows gathered in a troubled look. "A professional woman?"

At last those beautiful eyes softened and a smile played on his lips.

"Oh, my Kis Maria, I should have known you would not understand."

She laughed at the sound of his favorite nickname for her.

"I've been with a woman of the night. I've had sex with a

prostitute."

Her throat tightened. "Oh."

He sighed, his brow a little smoother now. "I can't stay. I had to tell you."

She shook her head. "You can stay!"

His frown faded to a little smile. "I must go. But read my paper."

Of course she would read it. "OK."

"Maybe you will understand."

"I will. I always understand you. You are the only one I understand."

A chuckle escaped his lips. "We'll see. But read it. And somehow, we need to talk."

"Yes! We must talk."

"Before I have to leave."

"Leave?" Ella gasped. "When are you leaving? Where are you going? I thought you would come home and be a lawyer."

"No, no. I can't stay here."

She gulped. "When are you leaving?"

"I don't know."

He pulled his watch from his vest pocket and looked at it. "I have to get back to the party."

He turned and was gone.

Ella looked at the open, empty door. He was here and now he was gone, like a dream that starts out well and turns dark. He was leaving Nagykanizsa. How would she survive without him? Of course, she had missed him when he was in Switzerland getting his law degree. And she had been disappointed when he had decided to get a sociology degree in Germany. She didn't even know what sociology was. She asked him why he wanted another degree. He said he had learned law was the foundation of society. But if that were true, to be a good lawyer one must understand society. So he needed to study sociology, which meant more years away from Nagykanizsa. During his long absences, Ella had cheered herself with the thought he would come home. Her lifelong friend would come home. He would not be gone forever.

But now? What would she do without him? She shuddered, shut the door, and sank down at the table, spreading his papers before her.

The typewritten letters – the 's's and 'e's lighter, the 'b's blotched and slightly higher than the others – ran across the page. How appropriate for the German to be typewritten, so formal, so modern. She read the title.

"The Sorrows of Sex"

She looked down at the table and thought. Was sex sorrowful? She didn't know. She had read of love and marriage and having babies, but she really hadn't thought much about sex. She should've known sex was an interesting topic, remembering how angry Mother had been when Ede had explained it to her. But it was not something she talked about with Ede, especially since he had been away these past years, and there were so many other things to talk about.

Her eyes wandered back to Ede's paper.

> *"Every country, every location has its special sorrows: cholera in England, the sleeping sickness in Africa, yellow fever in the Americas. And each social strata has its afflictions: hunger at the bottom, insecurity in the middle, boredom at the pinnacle. But there is one universal sorrow that afflicts all men: sex."*

Ella Reads the Essay

Ella looked up at the door where Ede had stood. This Ede was not the Ede she knew – the one who was quiet and patient and only talked when he had something important to say. This was a different Ede, as if the gypsies had taken his soul.

She banished thoughts of ladies of the night from her mind. She didn't even know if she had ever seen one. And she certainly did not want to talk about sex. Or think about sex. Ede had told her that what the stallion did to the mare on her grandmother's farm was what men did to women. It was even what gentlemen did to ladies. That was what Ede had said at the time. She had wished she had never asked him.

Now Ella remembered the hot day when the stallion was trotted into a corral with a mare. To this day, when she thought about sex she thought about those horses.

They were beautiful, both of them, the stallion coal black, the mare as silky red brown as a chestnut. The stallion stamped and snorted and reared, kicking up dirt, until Ella's eyes teared and the air smelled of hot dust and cut hay. Then, as if he just noticed the mare, he settled and walked over to her, pushing his muzzle next to hers and blowing in her nose. Ferenc had said horses didn't kiss. They blew into each other's nostrils. He had said that if Ella wanted her pony to love her, she should blow into his nostril. And she did.

So the stallion must have been loving the mare, because his nose was next to hers. And maybe she blew back, letting him know that she loved him too. The stallion moved his muzzle to the mare's neck and he nipped her, at her neck then at her withers. He thrust his nose under her belly. Now Ella could see his penis longer and straighter than she had ever seen before. He nipped the mare's hind quarter. She squawked, but stood still. He whirled around, rearing behind her. His chest settled on her rump, his front legs dangling on either side of her. His penis went into her. She stood still, her neck stretched forward, her head a little down. Then he was off her, his penis long and limp, like a cooked egg noodle. The mare nibbled hay. The stallion walked away.

Was that what Ede did to the lady of the night?

Ella pushed the image out of her mind.

She took a bite of stale bread which disintegrated in her mouth like dust, like the dust of the corral. She soaked the bread in her milk and took another bite, a soggy bite. She spread his paper in front of her. "*The Sorrows of Sex.*"

At least he seemed to agree with her. Sex was a misery, disgusting. At least it didn't seem to take too long.

She read the opening paragraph of Ede's paper again and considered it.

She was not hungry. Father was one of the wealthiest men in town. But he wasn't an aristocrat. And she definitely wasn't bored.

She read on.

"But there is one universal sorrow that afflicts all men: sex."

Really? Maybe it was different for men, because she was not miserable about sex. Then the next sentence:

"Sexual life is the most powerful factor in the individual and in society."

35

This couldn't be true. Love was important. In Huck Finn, the runaway Jim loved his family. Charles Darnay loved Lucie. But neither one of them seemed to be worried about sex.

She looked up, not really seeing the kitchen as she thought about the paper. She didn't understand, but she read further, because Ede had asked her to. He described an urgent need or desire. She felt no such thing. She had her wants: to read, to run, to talk with Ede about language and books. But she understood what she wanted and he was writing about a want she did not know.

She stared out the window. The afternoon's sunshine was dimming, making the room darker. She retrieved the oil lamp from her room and lit it, setting it on the table, so the yellow cone of light shone on Ede's paper. She settled on her chair and read again.

He wrote about the "silent sin." She didn't understand. It must be horrible and seemed to be secret, something that God could not forgive, that one must not talk about. It seemed to ruin his life. Some sin so powerful he could not control it, so horrible he was convinced he was bound for hell. That is what the priest told him.

He wrote about seeking relief from the chambermaid.

She gasped. Did Ede get relief from a chambermaid? One of his father's servants?

He wrote of the prostitutes. He said he had visited one.

He listed the horrors: money spent, blackmail, disease.

Ella heard voices on the front stairs. Had they come home already? She grabbed her books, dusting off crumbs, and rushed to her room, closing the door. She heard her family in the entry hall, Mother scolding Clara for getting her good dress dirty.

Ella placed her books and shawl in their hiding place, the

loose board in the floor that Ede had discovered so long ago. But where was Ede's essay?

She had left it on the kitchen work table.

Mother Finds the Essay

Therese's face was flushed when she entered the room. Maybe it was the wine. She held up a little bundle. "I've brought you something from the festivities. You must be hungry."

"Thank you!" Ella was ashamed of all her unkind thoughts. She bit into the apricot pinwheel, realizing that the dried bread, milk, and honey hadn't satisfied her.

"And next time," Therese said, "you can try on the dress a few days before an event. I can alter a dress easily enough."

"That is kind of you!" Ella looked at the frail woman, shorter than her and slight, her usually pale complexion rosy. "Very kind!"

"It's not that hard, and that way you don't have to miss the party." Her lips curved in a pretty smile, "Or dinner."

Ella nodded. Maybe this French companion, who she had thought of as a jailer, might turn out to be a friend. Maybe not a confident, not like Alexa, but at least she seemed to want to make Ella's life pleasant.

Before Ella could say thank you one more time, Clara came rushing into the room.

"It was so much fun, Mimi." Clara always called Ella Mimi, though Ella didn't know why or even when she started. "Oh, the dancing! The food! They even had a Csárdás band and dancers, and one of the dancers showed me some of their steps!"

Clara looked at Therese and pulled Ella down to her level,

whispering in her ear.

"And I danced with Ede!" She pushed Ella back a little, smiling broadly, the whisper again, "and he said not to worry, that he would see you before he leaves."

Clara jumped up. "Let me show you the Csárdás steps."

As she carefully placed her left foot in front of her right, Mother swept into the room.

"Out, Clara." Mother's face was flushed too, but Ella knew it wasn't wine. Her brow had gathered in a threatening cloud.

"Out, Clara. Time for bed!"

Ella saw Ede's pages in Mother's hand. Oh, this would be a gale.

"Therese, see to the kitchen. Her ladyship...." Mother waved her fingers in Ella's direction. "Didn't obey me. She has left dirty dishes and crumbs all over the table, and Cook is not here to clean up."

"Yes ma'am," Therese's knees dipped in a cursory curtsy before she rushed out.

Mother closed the door behind Therese. "So, what am I to do with you?" She leaned against the door. "You think you don't need to obey to me?"

Ella stared unblinkingly into her mother's eyes and didn't say a word.

"Leaving food in the kitchen, dirty dishes, milk, honey, all left out." Mother glowered at Ella. "I do believe you did that just to let me know you had disobeyed!"

Ella tried not to smile, but apparently failed.

"You think that is funny?"

Ella fixed her eyes on her mother.

"And then!" Mother lifted the hand that held Ede's paper and shook it. "And then! What do I find on the table, next to the crumbs and the dripped honey?"

Ella reached for the papers, her hand gripping one end, pulling. But her mother held tight and the sound of tearing roared in Ella's ears. The ripped pages fell to the floor.

"So, you didn't mean to leave this little piece of...." Mother looked at the sheets scattered at her feet. "This filth. How could you bring this filth into my house?"

Ella stared at the floor too. She wanted to gather up the pages, hoping to put them together. How could she have been so careless with Ede's work?

"How did this filth get into my house?"

Heat rose in Ella's cheeks. She wanted to scream at her mother, but she held her tongue.

"Was Ede here?"

Ella balled her hands and pressed her nails into her palms.

"I asked you a question Ella. Was Ede here?"

Ella did not move.

The sting of her mother's slap across her face felt good. She had provoked her mother to the slap. She had won.

"Answer me!"

"Yes." Ella smiled. "Yes, he was here."

Her mother sighed. "I think the only solution is a nunnery. You will come to no good unless you are kept under control. Obviously I cannot control you."

Her mother paced. "You are to stay in this room, until further notice." She stopped and turned on her heel and looked at Ella. "Do you understand?"

She nodded.

"And Ede." Her mother resumed her pacing between the window and the bed. "You are not permitted to see him." Again she turned to her daughter, hoping, Ella supposed, to see some anger or remorse, some indication she had broken her daughter's will. "Do you understand?"

Ella understood but she did not agree. She would find a way to see him.

Mother went back to her route between the window and the bed. "Maybe it is my fault. I should have never let him into this house, but I thought poor motherless child. I should have banned him after his blasphemy."

Mother stared at Ella. "Or was it your blasphemy? You were so young, not even confirmed yet. I suppose I can't blame you. But Ede knew exactly what he was doing. I should have banned him right then. Your father wouldn't hear of it, Ede's father being who he was. Your father told me it would cause a scandal. But what have we got now?" Her hollow laugh rang out as she nodded her head. "A scandal!"

She faced Ella, her finger pointing at the floor. "Pick up those dirty pages."

Ella did as she was told.

"Now hold them toward me."

Ella held them to her breast.

"Hold them toward me, unless you want me to burn you as well as that filth.

Ella clutched Ede's essay.

"Very well." As Mother found some matches next to the oil lamp on the bed cabinet, Ella slid a few of the scraps into her pocket. Mother turned and struck a match, pushing it through the distance between them. Her mother lit the pages, the yellow flame grew and scorched Ella's arm. Without thinking she dropped the papers and touched her burnt skin. She stared at her mother, unable to believe what she had done.

Mother snatched up the pages, holding a corner, and watched as the red-yellow tongue ate the white paper, curling the flimsy residue and turning it black. A smile flickered on her lips as she dipped the last of the flame in the water basin at the wash stand. Her skirts swished as she turned on her heel and left the room, pulling the door closed behind her.

Ella sank to her bed. She needed to see Ede. To explain what happened to his work. To find out what was wrong. To get him to stay in Nagykanizsa.

Needlecraft with Zsuzsi

The next day Ella watched Zsuzsi's fingers push the tatting scuttle over and under the thread held in her left hand, pulling it tight now and again. Zsuzsi might not be good at languages or math, but her fingers were clever, much smarter than Ella's.

Ella sighed. She had to find a way to see Ede.

"When you visit my house, I'll show you what Mutti gave me for my trousseau."

Ella wondered how her friend could talk while her hands performed their complicated ballet, the lace emerging from that dance. Her hands had a brain all their own.

"Oh darn." Ella dropped her knitting. "I see a mistake and it's a thousand rows back."

Zsuzsi looked up from her work. Placing her lace on her lap, she reached for Ella's knitting.

"See?" Ella pointed an inch below her current row.

"Ah, yes." Zsuzsi pulled a crotchet hook from her needlework kit and allowed the column of stitches above the mistake to unravel. "I'll fix it, no problem."

"Thanks."

"I saw Mother Mary Theresa at the wedding."

At the mention of the mother superior of the convent, Ella's stomach constricted. During her time at the convent school, Ella had spent some uncomfortable hours with Mother Mary Theresa. She had said something, she didn't remember what, that gave her teacher the impression she did not believe in God. Probably she had asked one too many questions. She was sent to Mother Mary Theresa, who used various methods to subdue the curious child. After that experience Ella had been careful not to ask questions and always to give the required answers. Rebelling against Mother was easy. Rebelling against the church, at least letting the sisters know of her rebellion, was much more work and much less fun.

"Mother Mary Theresa asked after you."

"She did?" Maybe Ella had played the good little girl too well.

"Yes. Sent her blessings."

Ella sat in silence while Zsuzsi worked. Ella thought that if she was confined to the house, without any books, at least it allowed her to make some progress on the trousseau. Or allowed Zsuzsi to help her make progress. Mother insisted on it, insisted that the things be made by Ella. How else would she know how to make these things when she had her own house to run?

The current project was a baby blanket. Ella didn't want a baby blanket. She didn't want a trousseau. She didn't want to get married. She didn't want to have a baby. She only wanted to see Ede.

Zsuzsi used the crochet hook to make the errant knit into a purl. "Did you hear? Father Joseph died?"

"Really?" Ella hated Father Joseph. Just as with Mother Mary Theresa, she had strategies for avoiding him.

"Uh-huh." Zsuzsi inspected the knitting. "It goes knit, knit, purl. Right?"

"Yes." Ella pointed to the pattern to help Zsuzsi.

Having determined the proper stitch sequence, Zsuzsi chattered on. "Anna says that maybe someone killed him." Anna was the cook at Zsuzsi's house.

"Are you serious?"

"Very." Picking up the next stitch she looked up from her work. "Anna's from Kiskanizsa and she says Dragica...."

"Dragica?" Ella had heard the name discussed by Maid and Cook. She had even once overheard Mother whispering the name to one of her friends.

"Dragica." Zsuzsi smiled knowingly. "The Croat herbalist said that Father Joseph did unnatural things. Evil things."

"What things?"

"She didn't say. But Dragica said that God wanted him dead because of those things."

Ella shrugged. Zsuzsi liked to talk about the result of others' sins. Ella thought she made most of it up and she wanted to talk about something else. She knew just the thing. "You were saying you got something new for your trousseau?"

"Oh yes! Mutti bought me the most exquisite sugar shaker."

"That's kind of her."

"It's silver, with etched patterns."

"It must be beautiful." Ella thought it must have been expensive – expensive, and the etchings would make it hard to keep clean.

Zsuzsi completed the repair and handed the knitting back to Ella.

"It is beautiful." She took up the lace and the scuttle. "Mutti thinks I have everything I really need now. So, she's getting these beautiful extras."

"Mmmm." Ella was sure she didn't have everything she needed. Father had provided the everyday linens, dishes, the crystal, and the silver utensils, but Mother refused to get any extras until Ella had completed all kinds of needlecraft projects, the baby blanket being one of them.

"Now all I need is a husband!" Zsuzsi giggled. "By the way, I danced with Ede at the wedding. He's handsome, but too young, don't you think?"

Ella's knitting dropped to her lap, several stitches slipping off the needle. She cleared her throat, pushing the thought of Ede married to Zsuzsi out of her mind. Would he like talking about babies, silver, weddings and funerals?

"He's too young."

Most men didn't get married until they were in their thirties. Ella had asked her father why. He said a man had to be established, had to make enough money to be able to support a family before he could marry. It meant that girls like Zsuzsi and Ella would marry disgusting old men.

"Mutti had Mrs. Farkas visit the other day. I had tea with her."

Mrs. Farkas, a small slight woman with a disdainful look, was the matchmaker. Ella thought the name appropriate. Farkas, wolf, cunning, dangerous. But she was really more like a fox than a wolf. Her red brown hair was the color of fox fur and she came sniffing around, like a fox tracking his prey.

"What was that like?"

"Nothing special. We talked about normal things: church, who's getting married, who had babies...."

Zsuzsi was being put through her paces. The matchmaker wanted to make sure she was a proper young woman.

"But Mutti said that maybe they would look in Vienna."

That would make sense, Ella thought. Zsuzsi's German was much better than her Hungarian, but she wouldn't say so.

"Would you like living in Vienna?"

Her friend shrugged. "Why not?"

Didn't it matter what Zsuzsi would like? They worked on their projects in silence.

"Why didn't you come to the wedding?"

Ella considered telling Zsuzsi the truth. That was not a good idea; the whole town would know five minutes after she left.

"I wasn't feeling well."

"What? Was it your time?"

Ella nodded and smiled. That was as good a lie as any.

"Too bad. It was fun. Lots of people asked where you were."
She grinned. "Ede asked where you were."

Ella's Discovery

Ella fished the scraps of Ede's paper from her pocket. Just three. She studied the words, but there was not a complete sentence to be had on them. She closed her eyes. Did he have a copy or had her mother destroyed the only one? How could she have been so careless? Yes, her books were precious, but there were other copies of those books. But this paper, which Ede had written, and no matter how strange – Ella stopped herself from agreeing with her mother, that Ede was strange – it was far more valuable.

She leaned on the bed and looked at the floor, remembering how the black ashes of what had been Ede's words, his words of anguish, had lain scattered. Her eye swept back and forth, wishing she could undo the fire, that she could hold those pages in her hand. Her eye stalled on a white corner peeking out from under the bed cabinet. Was that a page that escaped? She picked it up.

Instead of Ede's manuscript, Ella held a design, drawn on heavy card stock and done in black ink and watercolor, the paint blending shades of blue, from the lightest sky to midnight so dark it was almost black. She recognized the work. Miklos drew the most beautiful designs and this one was one of his, graceful arcs of stems with flowers and hearts, all resting in a vase. Ella marveled at its simple elegance.

Even with Miklos's anger, nastiness, teasing, he could melt her heart with his designs. Why was this one in her room?

She turned the card over and read:

Ma chère T,
Avec toi, je suis moi.
Je t'aime.
                    M

Ella laughed. Her brother was taking French lessons from Therese! Maybe he was learning more than French? They said the best way to learn a language was from a lover. Maybe that flush on Therese's cheek was more than wine?

Ella slid the card and the remains of Ede's paper into her pocket. What would Mother say to those goings on? She knew the routine. Therese would be dismissed, as if the affair were her fault. No one would say a word about Miklos or even why Therese was let go.

She fingered the card in her pocket. As far as she knew, there was no affair. Perhaps Miklos was just trying to seduce Therese, and she was trying to keep her distance. The blush after the wedding might have been suppressed anger at having been accosted by her employer's son.

But if Therese were angered by Miklos's approach, she would have destroyed the note. She would never have brought this piece of evidence into the house. No. Ella was sure. Therese and Miklos were doing something that should not be done. Maybe Therese hoped to change her role from servant to mistress.

What would that mean for Ella?

Not good. Newly minted mistresses were notorious for being mean to spinster sisters-in-law. Ella planned never to marry. Never to become like Mother. She hoped to somehow wheedle her way into the business, maybe by making herself indispensable. Helping Father with the books. She had asked to see the books, but so far Father had refused with a "Don't worry your pretty head with such things. It will make you ugly."

How Ella wished she had been born a boy. If she were a boy, she would understand all the things Miklos and Father discussed at the dinner table. She would know how to design tools, she would understand why the drills her father made were superior, and how the Wright brothers could make planes fly. If only she were a boy!

She smiled inwardly. Father had said it was a pity that she was not a boy, because she would have been a great help in his business, with her handle on math and her practicality. When he had said that, she had asked him why she couldn't be a partner in his business. He had laughed, shook his head and patted her hair. Proper ladies, he told her, had families and raised children. They did not run businesses.

But this was no time to dream about impossibilities. Best to think about the current problem. Best to nip Therese in the bud, before she could rise. Miklos was young to be marrying, just like Ede. But sometimes men married that young, if their livelihood was assured. Miklos would inherit the family business, so if he really "t'aimed T", he might marry. She must tell Mother and get rid of Therese. That way no one would be available to mind her. That way she would find a way to see Ede.

The door creaked open and Therese appeared, her face pale. "Ma'am is in such a mood!"

Ella nodded.

"Again she was raging about Ede, how you are not to see him."

Ella nodded again.

Therese looked into Ella's eyes. "Is he your sweetheart?"

"No, just a friend." The only true friend she'd ever had. The only truthful friend she'd ever had.

"Why does your mother not want you to see him?"

"Mother gets into these strange moods."

This was true. Some of Mother's actions seemed random. This particular one had its reasons, but Ella wouldn't explain and she was sure her Mother wouldn't either, not wanting the world to know that Ella had seen such, as her mother put it, filth.

"Seems a pity." Therese smiled. "He seemed like a nice young man. Handsome. And he wanted to know why you had not come."

"What did you say?"

"Ma'am instructed me to say that you were ill."

Ella nodded. She studied Therese, her slight figure, her wispy hair. She was not a bad person. She just had a job that required her to be a jailer. It wasn't her fault. It seemed unfair to get her dismissed. She had a right to steal a bit of happiness. She had told Ella that her child had died and shortly after, her husband had died too, leaving her without money. Her family was poor and she had come here because she had nowhere else to go.

Still, Ella had to see Ede. He seemed to be anguished or ill. Something was wrong. She had to see Ede. And maybe, if Therese were not here she could manage to sneak a visit with him, while Mother was not minding her.

And then she realized she had a better plan. She had a plan that would guarantee a visit with Ede. She withdrew the card from her pocket so that Therese could see it.

The Deal

Therese reached for the card, her lips pressed together, her brows contracted.

"That is mine." Her ragged voice cut through the silence. "Give it to me."

"Ah, but I found it."

Ella was being mean, but she didn't care. She had to see Ede and that justified her actions. Besides, Therese was Mother's servant, an extension of Mother's discipline. Rebellion against Therese was the same as rebellion against Mother.

She waved the card. "I found it and now it is mine."

Therese stepped back, her pale face calm. "You want money?"

Ella hadn't considered that. "No. Not money." She sat on the bed, pocketing the card. "I can understand being in love."

Therese spat out the words. "Who says I'm in love?"

Ella chuckled. "If you were not in love, you wouldn't care about the card."

Therese shook her head. "Miklos writing a silly card says nothing about me." She shrugged and scrunched her face, her lips turned down. "Who understands men? They have their little desires, which fade quickly enough. A wise woman ignores them." She smoothed her skirt. "A good lesson for you, Miss."

Ella considered again whether this "affair" was one sided. Was Therese not in love with Miklos? But if not, why had she saved the card? Maybe she hadn't. Maybe Miklos had just given her the card and she hadn't had time to destroy it.

It really didn't matter. Ella needed this tool. She must see Ede.

"If Mother sees this...." Ella waved the card like a weapon. It was a gamble. Maybe Therese truly didn't care for Miklos, in which case his advances would mean she would have to leave in any case. Maybe she planned to destroy the note and say she must leave, asking for a reference. Ella studied Therese's flushed face.

"But... if I never found it, she'd never know."

Therese nodded and looked down, defeated.

"I have a deal," Ella said.

Therese didn't move.

Ella's voice was silky smooth. "One I think you will like."

Therese looked up, her eyebrow raised.

Ella smiled. "One where you will have more time for Miklos, if that is what you want. Or, if you'd rather, more time for yourself."

The room was silent except for the distant clatter of a cart rolling down Fő út.

Clara Helps

Clara ran into Ella's room. "Mother's in a state!" She laughed. "She's breathing fire!"

"Come sit next to me and tell me all about it." Ella slid over on the bed, making more room for her sister. "Did she say what was wrong?"

"Nothing I understood."

Clara sat as directed and swung her feet back and forth. "Something about filth, dirt."

She stopped and scrunched her face in concentration. "I think she said something about smut."

Her face relaxed and looked up at her sister. "Mimi, are you in trouble again?"

"Always!" Ella looked down at the youngster and ran her fingers through her sister's silky hair. How was it that Clara never seemed to be the cause of Mother's concern? Maybe Ella used up all the "concern" Mother had.

Clara grinned. "What happened?"

Ella considered whether to tell Clara. She had always been open with Clara. Pretty open, anyhow. But this plan of hers was delicate. Might the child reveal too much to Mother, maybe unwittingly. But Clara could be her ally, her means of communication. She could use Therese or Miklos, but she didn't trust them, even with her new weapon. She trusted Clara more.

"Ede wrote a paper."

"What's wrong with that?" Bewilderment flooded Clara's

face. "I have to write for Moni." Moni was her tutor.

"Mother didn't like what was in the paper."

"What was in it?"

"Apparently filth, dirt, and smut."

Clara laughed. "Really?"

Now was not the time to debate that issue. "I'm not sure."

"You didn't read it?"

"Mother burned it before I had a chance to understand it."

"It must have been bad."

"That is why I need you to help me." She searched Clara's face. "You must do as I say and do it exactly." She saw Clara's look of concentration. "Otherwise we will both be in big trouble."

Clara nodded, holding Ella's stare. "OK."

"I have a note here for Ede. When you go out with Moni tomorrow afternoon, stop by his house and leave it with the cook."

Clara squinted, apparently considering the plan. "Is it OK that Moni knows that I am leaving a note for Ede?"

"Maybe not. Good thinking, little sleuth." Ella was stumped. How to get word to Ede to meet her? "See if you can find Ede. He might be at the café." This seemed unlikely. Maybe she should have Therese handle the communication after all. But she just didn't trust Therese enough.

Clara slid off the bed, turned to her sister, her face bright. "I know. We'll go to the market this afternoon. Ede's cook will be there. I will give her the note."

"Moni goes to the market? Doesn't Cook go to the market?"

"Sure, but Moni likes talking to her friends. They meet at the market. She lets me wander while she's gossiping. If I can't find Ede's cook, I can run over to his house and leave it with the maid."

"You can do that?"

"Sure. It's boring hanging around while Moni is chattering. She's used to me wandering and won't notice."

Ella smiled. Clara was a clever little thing.

"What's the note about?"

"Oh, Clara, you don't need to know." Clara's face fell. "Besides, it's best that you don't know. If something goes wrong, then you can truly say you don't know what it was all about." Clara's face still tinted with disappointment. "Like a true spy, who doesn't know everything, in case he is caught."

Clara beamed.

Apparently she liked being a spy.

Ede and Ella Talk

It had all gone according to Ella's plan. Therese had convinced Mother that Ella needed fresh air and exercise. Clara had delivered the note, and now, at last Ella and Ede walked deep into the woods, silent but for the crunch of leaves underfoot, the twitter of birds in the trees, and the chatter of an unhappy squirrel. Ella didn't want to tell Ede about his burnt essay until they were settled and she could study his face. Finally they turned and looked at the path they had taken, the main road hidden by the green leaves and tree trunks. Ede spread a blanket he carried and they settled on it.

Ella's hands were sweaty with worry. "Did you hear? Mother burned your manuscript."

"Yes, yes." His eyes gleamed as he chortled. "Miklos told me. He enjoyed telling me." Ede stretched.

"But, is it...." She tried again. "I mean, is that the only copy you had?"

"No, my dear Ella. I have other copies."

"I was so foolish to leave it where Mother could see."

"Ella, look at me." He lifted her chin with his finger, holding her gaze. "It is all right." He grinned. "Maybe it is even good that Auntie saw the paper."

Ella blinked. "Good? She forbids me to see you and that's good?"

"Not that she forbids our meeting. That's not good. But things are changing and she needs to be prepared."

Ella shook her head. "I don't understand. Not at all. You say such strange things. Are you OK?"

"Of course." His smile shone, his old self-confident smile, so different from his frazzled face the day of the wedding. "Relax. We have lots to talk about and the martyred paper is not important. Relax so we can have a good talk."

"But when you came...."

"Yes, I know. But I had to tell you and it was difficult."

She nodded and pulled a strand of her auburn hair loose from her hairpins. She twiddled the lock between her fingers.

"Why?"

"Why did I have to tell you or why was it difficult?"

"Yes." Her fingers busily twisted her hair.

"Why I had to tell you is a long story." A little smile lingered on his lips but the green in his hazel eyes shone, which she knew meant he was serious. "A very long story, which I hope to tell you now."

"OK."

"Why it is difficult is easy. I am ashamed. It is difficult to confess a shameful act. At least for me. Don't you think?"

"I don't admit shameful acts." Her stare was unblinking. "I'll tell you that I don't commit shameful acts."

His laugh billowed into the warm afternoon. "I'm not sure of that. Your letting Auntie see my paper, were you not ashamed of that?"

She nodded.

"Ah, well, but the statement is pure Ella." He chuckled and looked past the trees toward the road. "I love pure Ella."

His face, no trace of the smile, turned back to her. "I love you, Ella."

"And I love you too, Ede. You know that."

"No, Ella. I don't mean that. Not love like a brother. Well, yes." He stopped and looked away and a wistful chuckle escaped from his lips. "I do love you like a brother."

His gaze turned back to her. "But I want to love you like a husband."

"Oh." She felt the blood come to her cheeks. "Isn't that something you are supposed to arrange with a matchmaker?" She swallowed. "Or at least ask Father?"

"I don't need a matchmaker. I don't care what Uncle will say. I care what you will say. I will not be married to Uncle Weisel. I will be married to you."

"Oh." She didn't want to marry.

He repeated her oh, a sad quiet echo.

"Ede." She didn't know what to say. "Ede, I can't imagine life without you."

"That's good."

"But you said you were leaving."

"Yes, yes. That is part of the long story." He took in a deep breath and put on a brave smile. "I got ahead of myself. This is almost as difficult as confessing a sin."

"Is it?" She leaned back on her elbows, happy that the question of marriage had been postponed.

"I've finished my education. I'm ready to start off in life. When I first left for school I thought I would be a lawyer, so I got a law degree." He hugged his knees to his chest. "But when I was in Switzerland and Germany, well, I learned something more than law."

"Like meeting with ladies of the night?"

"Oh, Ella, I do love you." He scanned her face. "That is why I told you about my sins. I wanted to prove to myself I could tell you anything."

"You can."

"I believe you will listen to anything, but it is also hard to tell you some things." He tilted his head. "Anyhow, no, not to meet ladies of the night. Hungary, even Nagykanizsa, has ladies of the night, in case you didn't know. I didn't need to go to Leipzig to learn that."

Ella sensed impatience in his voice. "I'm sorry."

"Never mind." Again the brave smile. It was like the smile of the wedding day. Not a happy smile. "I learned there are better societies, better ways for a country to be run, better than feudal Hungary."

"Feudal? The serfs were freed long ago."

Ella searched for the date, but winning freedom was complicated and she couldn't remember the details.

He snorted. "Yes, yes. On paper the serfs are free. But in reality...." He shrugged. "The aristocrats own a huge proportion of the land. They own whole villages. And whoever lives on the land those aristocrats own...." He frowned. "They might as well be serfs."

"Really?"

"Sure. Few people are allowed to vote, and what voting there is, is open. Everyone knows how you vote." He frowned and shook his head. "You vote as the aristocrats want you to vote. They might as well be kings."

"Are you going to another country then? To a better country?"

Ella was uncertain about marrying Ede, but living in another country sounded wonderful, exciting, maybe even worth marrying.

"No, no." Ede sighed and stretched his legs out. "I want to help my country, my backward Hungary, become a better country."

"How?"

"I'm not sure, but it must change." He sighed and looked in the distance.

A squirrel scampered across the leaves.

Ede resettled on the blanket. "I know an aristocrat who bragged about taking a horsewhip to his stable boy. The authorities looked the other way."

He looked back at Ella, his lips compressed. "And I don't think that's the worst of it"

Ella gulped. "Really?"

He nodded and expelled a breath. "The counts and barons own huge forests, their private hunting grounds. The peasants are not allowed in those lands, not to collect wood to keep warm in winter, or to pick berries and mushrooms to supplement their meals, and certainly not to kill a deer so that their children might have some meat."

"Like in the song Alexa used to sing?" Ella sang:

Ah my Geordie will be hanged in a golden chain
Tis not the chain of many
Stole sixteen of the king's royal deer,
and he sold them in Bohenny.

Ede scoffed. "Oh, I think your Geordie was a lucky fellow. He was to be hanged by a golden chain, so he was a noble. And he wasn't going to eat the deer, he was going to sell them."

His smile was crooked, ironic. "No, Ella, our peasants don't get enough to eat. They are, according to what I have read, slowly starving because they aren't paid enough to feed their families. And if, out of desperation, a peasant mother enters a noble's forest, to find food for her children, that noble can do with her as he pleases. He might even murder her."

Ella couldn't believe this, but he nodded, pursing his lips. "A person who does such things is despicable. A country that allows such acts to go unpunished is...." He shook his head with a shudder. "And think about Father Joseph."

"What about him?"

"When I needed consolation most. When I needed to understand myself, to forgive myself, he convinced me of my guilt."

Ede closed his eyes and sneered. "I believe he enjoyed listening to my confession, that he was, in fact, committing the very sin I was confessing, while I cried bitter tears."

Ella didn't understand, but Ede's face was pale and his eyes, now open, told her he wanted to say no more, so she was silent.

He exhaled, as if he were trying to expel his gloom. "But maybe I should be grateful to him. He showed me how false the church is."

Looking down, Ede picked up a leaf by its stem and twirled it. His eyes returned to Ella. His voice was harsh. "How evil the church is."

"The church is evil?"

"Yes, Ella. The Church is powerful and it works not for the good of the people, but for its own good."

Ella's hand covered her throat. What would Mother do if she heard him now?

A sad smile spread across his lips. "Yes, Ella. The church is a huge problem, along with the aristocracy." He tossed the leaf across the blanket. "And think about women."

"Women?"

"Yes, women." Ede picked up another leaf from next to the blanket. "Remember our aristocrat who horsewhipped his stable boy?"

Ella nodded.

"He likes to talk about the peasant lasses who await the hunters after a hard day of slaying deer."

"Await?"

"Yes, those barons and counts find naked peasant girls warming their beds when they retire."

Ede tore the leaf in half.

"Do you suppose those little girls, because they are really not women yet, have a choice?"

Ede shredded the leaf with his fingers.

"No. They do as their master tells them." Holding his hand up, he let the shredded leaf fall to the blanket.

Ella bit her knuckle. "It can't be true. Not now."

Ede stared at her. "It's true. Now. Our Hungarian aristocracy, they are as cruel as Eastern tyrants."

Ella inhaled the musty forest smells, trying to make peace with Ede's words. Could this really be her Hungary?

Ede leaned back on his elbows, sighing. "The aristocrats abusing girls, that is the most dramatic of the problems facing women. But there are others. Problems facing all Hungarian women, even if they are countesses. And perhaps these problems are just as important."

Ella closed her eyes and shook her head, trying to make room for more atrocities. "Which others?"

"For example, most of the education system is closed to women."

He looked at her, his face less strained. "Just think about yourself, Ella. You're smart. Even without a proper education, you've learned so much."

Ede shrugged, lifting his hands, palms up. "If you had a proper education you could do anything you wanted, follow any career...."

She had always thought it would have been better if she had been born a boy, that she was not womanly because she was interested in things boys were supposed to be good at. She had never considered that the problem was society rather than the way she felt. But here Ede was saying it was society.

"How I wish I could have gone to gymnasium."

Instead of the convent school with its needle crafts, she would have liked to be with the boys in their school, their gymnasium, learning Latin and Greek, algebra and trigonometry.

Ede grinned. "And university."

She looked at him in surprise. "And university?"

"Of course. You would study languages."

She let this idea settle.

"And women aren't the only ones denied an education, even just a rudimentary education. In fact many Hungarians can't read or write." He shook his head. "How can we be a wealthy modern country if people are illiterate?"

"It's not like that in Germany?"

"Yes and no." He tilted his head toward his raised shoulder. "But not nearly as bad."

Ella hugged her legs to her chest and rested her chin on them. "But how do you change these things?"

"I'm not sure." Ede shrugged. "But I start by going to Budapest."

"Why Budapest?"

"The capitol, where the power is. And I have the names of some people who think as I do. People who think there are ways to make Hungary more like the Western countries, less like the East. All Hungarians, men and women, need to be treated equally. The government should be for the people, not the other way around." He sighed. "We should be more like England. More like the United States."

They sat in silence, a little breeze cooling the air and rustling the leaves.

"It sounds important. Important and wonderful. But I don't

want you to leave."

He locked his eyes on hers. "You could come too."

She stared at him.

He held her gaze, no hint of a smile on his serious face. "It is time that I marry."

Ella found this unlikely. "Most men don't marry until they are in their thirties. You're only 24."

"But I don't want to be like most men. And I'm lucky. I am well off. When my father died I received a large inheritance. "

Ella thought of Ede's father's death, just last year. Ede had come home for the funeral and had stayed a while. When she had asked what it was like to have a father die, Ede had shrugged and said that Ella's father had been more of a parent to him than his own father. Perhaps that was true.

She sighed. "OK. I understand. You can marry."

Even though it was possible, Ede's desire to be married seemed strange. It seemed so sudden.

"But why do you want to marry?"

"The proper answer for a gentleman would be, because I love you Ella and I want to marry you."

She laughed. "But you are not a proper gentleman."

"No." His eyes twinkled. "You taught me to be ungentlemanly. Do you remember?"

"Of course."

How could she forget the ball, the fire, and how angry she was when he tried to protect her?

Usually when Ede reminded her of this incident he laughed, but now his hazel eyes were soft and serious. "The truth is I do love you, Ella, and I do want to marry you."

She grinned. "So you turned into a proper gentleman?"

"No. I love you. That is true." He blushed. "But it is also true that if I go to Budapest without you then the sorrows of sex will rule me. I need to conquer them. The best way is to be married."

She looked down and ran her hand across the grass. She wanted not to think about marriage.

"I know. You are young. Just 18."

She nodded.

"But you would make my plan perfect. You are my family, Ella. You and Uncle and Auntie and Miklos. But it is really you, only you who are my family. I cannot go to Budapest without you.'

"But what would I do? Have children?"

"Yes, yes. We would have children."

"Oh." Ella thought of her mother.

"But not only children, Ella. You can help with my plan."

"How?"

"I'm not sure. We'd have to figure that out." Ede took his watch from his vest pocket, looked at it and replaced it. "But we must go now. We're late and we must meet Therese and Miklos."

She stood, brushing the grass from her skirt.

He stood, placing his hands on her shoulders so that he could look into her eyes. "I know you are young. I know this is a surprise. But think about it. I will not talk to Uncle until you have said yes." He caressed her cheek, and, leaning down, placed a gentle kiss on her lips.

She inhaled his scent and clasped his hand. She wanted another kiss, but he led her to the path, back to Miklos and Therese, back to Mother's grim house.

A Misunderstanding

Therese seemed more relaxed about the next meeting, maybe because the first had gone smoothly. They had planned to go to city park this time and meet Miklos and Ede in the woods not far from the entrance.

Their beaus were waiting for them. Ede and Ella headed in one direction, Miklos and Therese in another.

Ede opened the blanket next to a little stone shelter and they settled on it. Ella stared into his eyes. "The answer is no."

"OK." Ede's eyes held hers, a serious even a stern gaze. "I accept it. The answer is no." He looked past her, through the trees of the park. "But I won't accept the no until you have explained it."

"I don't want to have children."

His chuckle seemed to expel his gloom. "I see. You don't want to have children now."

"No." Ella shook her head. "I don't want to have children ever."

"You might change your mind...."

"No." Her throat tightened. She didn't want to argue. "No children ever."

"OK. So we won't have children. Will you marry me if we don't have children?"

"But then we wouldn't...." She couldn't help grinning at him, because she knew she was poking his tender spot. "We won't solve the sorrows of sex."

"Oh." He let the word draw out, a smile on his lips. "I see the problem. There is a little misunderstanding here."

"There is? I thought you wanted to get married now to solve that problem."

"I do." His smile grew wider. "But one can have intercourse without getting pregnant."

"You can have intercourse...." She stared at him.

"Yes, Kis Maria, you can."

"But I thought the whole point of sex was to make children."

"Well, it is true as far as nature goes. But there are ways around nature."

"What are they?"

"There are a number of ways. Not hard. Not complicated. We can talk about them later. Right now, I want to know if you will marry me if we don't have children.

"Oh." She had thought so hard about this problem and had realized her reluctance centered on having children. But if that was not a problem, why shouldn't she marry Ede? Still it made her uneasy.

"'Oh' is not an answer to the question." He clipped his words, like a teacher waiting for the proper response. "Will you marry me?"

"I...." She looked down and pulled at the grass. "I don't know."

"OK. Then tell me why you don't want to have children."

"Because... well, look at Mother. She has children and she is angry all the time and does nothing interesting. She never laughs. She just complains."

"So you think if you have children you will be like your mother?"

"Of course...."

Again the sweet laugh.

"It's easy for you to laugh because you aren't...." She didn't want to say it, but she did, "Because you aren't a woman."

"But women like children."

Ella exhaled and pursed her lips. "That's what men say."

"You like Clara."

"That's different."

"I don't know. Is it?"

"Yes. Because Clara isn't my child." She exhaled an exasperated huff. "I don't know. I want something else than children. I don't want to lose my mind. I want to think and...."

He looked confused. "You won't stop thinking if you have a child...."

"I don't know...."

"OK. So you don't know. That's fair, but will you marry me if we don't have children?"

Ella was silent, not knowing what she wanted.

"I think you will like being married to me."

She flashed him a smile. Being with him all the time, what else could she want?

"We would have lots of thinking to do." His eyes shone. "You will meet interesting people. People who want to change Hungary."

"What happens if I don't agree with you?"

They had argued about abstract things, but maybe she would think he was wrong about something real, something important.

Again the melody of his laugh.

"Of course, you will think I'm wrong. And we will argue. That's the way to find solutions. That's the way we've always worked, ever since you were four. That's why I love you."

Ella put a blade of grass between her thumbs, placed her lips to her thumbs and blew. A razzing sound interrupted the silence. She dropped the grass and looked up at him. She wanted to be with him forever. She wanted to say yes. She thought about all their discussions, about whether it was better to be a serf than a slave, about how Twain's English was the same language as Dickens' English, whether gypsies were evil or just misunderstood. Going to Budapest, the capitol! Talking to Ede about his plan. Talking to people who made a difference. Being part of something important. Was that the something she wanted? Yes. It was. That was the inexplicable something she wanted. She looked into his beautiful eyes.

"Yes."

"Yes?" He swallowed. "Yes, you will marry me?"

"Yes."

"Oh!"

He slid over so his hip touched hers.

"Oh, yes!"

He brushed an auburn strand of hair behind her ear. He kissed her.

"It will be heaven. You will see."

A tremor thrummed through her. She touched her cheek against his and then stared deep into his eyes. Her lips brushed his and returned to his again.

As she inhaled his scent, her throat tightened.

She felt like laughing and crying at the same time.

His laugh boomed.

"It will be heaven. You will love it."

He wrapped his arms around her.

"Maybe, when you get older, you will even change your mind about children."

Therese's Problem

Therese, who had seemed so carefree yesterday, when they had met with their beaus, sniffled as she wiped her eyes. "I'm not feeling well."

"What's wrong?"

"Just my time."

Strange, Ella thought. She had cramps when she had her period, but it wasn't so bad. Maybe it was different if one were small and slight like Therese. Ella was not ungainly, but tall and slender. She had rose in her cheeks, especially when she ran, or rode, or swam, or sledded, or skated. All things Mother discouraged. Mother wanted her to stay indoors. She thought young ladies should be pale, like Therese. But if being pale meant your period made it too painful to go out, to meet with your lover, then she'd rather have rose in her cheeks and look like a peasant.

Ella leaned against the bed. "But we must at least go out to tell Miklos and Ede we cannot stay. And you must come, because Mother won't allow me to go out alone."

"No, no." Therese tucked her handkerchief into her sleeve. "I cannot go out."

"Maybe Mother will let me go out with Clara," Ella wondered whether this would be a good idea. She didn't want Clara to know more than she already did.

"No, it will be all right." Therese sat up straighter, taking control of the situation. "They will wait and when we don't come, Miklos will come home to find out what's wrong."

71

Ella didn't like the idea. "I'll go with Clara."

Therese explained the situation to Mother and suggested that Clara could chaperone in her stead. To Ella's surprise, Mother agreed. Ella and Clara rushed to the park where Ede and Miklos were waiting.

Ede jumped up from the bench. "You're late."

"Oh, look who's here," Ella said, pretending this was an accidental meeting. Surely Clara would smell a rat. But Clara was smart and could keep a secret. At least Ella hoped so.

"Where's Therese?" Miklos asked.

"She wasn't feeling well, so Mother allowed me to go out with Clara." Ella met eyes with her brother, hoping he would take the hint.

"What's wrong?" Miklos held Ella's gaze.

"I'm not sure. Maybe you should check on her. She's at home."

Miklos turned toward home, his steps quick and determined.

"Well, I can walk with you two lovely ladies," Ede said, placing his hand on Ella's elbow and guiding them away from home.

"I don't think it would be a good idea," Ella said.

"Just the three of us? Who could object to the three of us taking a little stroll?"

"Mother?" Clara chimed in.

Ella laughed. "Smart little sister I have!"

"Yes, yes," Ede ruffled Clara's hair, "But I will tame Mother, just as I will tame Clara, and even you, Ella."

When Ella returned home, she found Therese in their shared room, hugging Miklos in a tight embrace. Her cheeks were red and shone with tears. Ella started to back out of the room.

"No," Miklos said, untangling himself from Therese. "I must

go now. I have things I must arrange."

Ella scanned her brother's face. His bloodshot eyes avoided her gaze. Therese was not the only one who had been crying.

"Stay with Therese." Miklos pleaded. "She needs company right now."

Ella twisted the strand of hair at her right ear. "Of course."

Miklos bolted out the door.

Ella, by pure instinct, sat next Therese on the bed. She didn't like this fragile French woman, but they shared a secret, and she knew she must be kind. "I could get Cook to bring you some tea."

"No!" Therese's swollen eyes searched Ella's. "No one must see me like this."

"If you would like, I'll get you some tea."

"It's not necessary." Therese sat up straighter and, pulling her handkerchief from her sleeve, wiped her face. "Maybe, if you could get some cold water, so I could freshen up?"

"Of course."

When Ella returned with a jug of water, Therese was putting some things in a little satchel, the satchel Ella had not seen since Therese's arrival six weeks ago.

"Are you leaving?"

Therese turned toward Ella. Her lower lip trembled. "I hope not."

Ella glanced at the satchel, as if to ask why she seemed to be packing.

"I need to see the herbalist."

"The herbalist?" Was this Dragica, the woman Zsuzsi mentioned?

Therese ignored Ella's apparent question. "Miklos thinks that she will be able to make me feel better. He's gone to find her and arrange for me to see her."

"What's wrong?"

"Oh, nothing that important." Therese said, pouring water into the basin. She took a cloth from the hook, dipped it into the basin and squeezed the excess from the cloth.

"Nothing you need to worry about."

Marketing with Clara

The next day Ella and Clara walked along Fő út toward Erzsébet Square where the market was held. Cook was busy and Therese did not feel well, so Mother had allowed Ella to go as long as Clara accompanied her.

"Mimi, why doesn't Mother want you to see Ede?" Clara's question was a demand. The magic of being a spy must have been worn thin by the child's curiosity.

"Mother said that if we met Ede we were to leave immediately, no matter what. Why?"

"Mother is mad at Ede."

"But it is more than that." Clara stopped walking and stared at Ella. "Mother didn't forbid me from seeing him. Just you."

Ella considered what to say without getting everyone in trouble. "It's hard to explain."

Clara continued her defiant stare, waiting for a real explanation.

"Clara, if I tell you more, you must swear that you will tell no one. Not Moni, not Miklos, Not Cook or Maid or Father. And especially not Mother."

Clara's lower lip protruded and her brows furrowed.

"No. Clara. I mean it. You must swear!"

"Of course." Clara's words were staccato. "I'm not a snitch."

"I know, but sometimes you let on, just because you don't think of the consequences of what you say."

"OK." Clara sing-songed. She took in Ella's intent stare and her voice grew serious. "I swear. I won't say anything."

"Not even anything close to the topic?" Ella saw that Clara was listening intently. "Like talking about Ede's paper?"

"Ede's paper?"

"Yes, Ede's paper. But first you must say you won't talk about anything even closely related to what I tell you now."

"OK." Clara nodded, her eyes serious.

"Well, the first thing is sex." They started walking again. "But not a word to anyone. Otherwise Mother might not even allow you to see me."

Clara stopped and shook her head. "She couldn't do that. You're my sister."

That was the argument Ella should have used to start. "Yes. But Mother wants to keep certain things secret. From you. And from me. And she is willing to separate us."

Clara nodded again.

"So about sex."

They reached the market place and sat on a bench to finish Clara's first sex education lesson.

"So why does Mother not allow you to see Ede?"

"Because Ede wrote a paper about sex, about how much men want to have sex."

"But I thought you had sex because you love the other person."

"I don't know." Ella let out a little snort. She had had the same notion. "According to Ede's paper that is not true."

"Oh."

Ella could see Clara was digesting this information.

"So," Clara said, "Ede wants to have sex before he's married."

Ella drew in a deep breath. This was blunt. She hadn't thought of it in this way. But it was true.

Clara's face darkened in confusion. "Does that make him a bad person? A sinful person? Isn't there a commandment that says 'Do not lust'?"

"But there is also a commandment 'Do not lie'. What do you do when one commandment tells you to do something and another commandment tells you to do the opposite?"

"I don't know. What do you do?"

"I don't know either."

Clara looked off in the distance, biting at her thumb nail. Her curiosity seemed diverted to moral dilemmas, a more comfortable place from Ella's point of view.

"I'll buy you a poppy-seed cake and then I'll get our provisions."

"OK." Clara's face was bright with a huge smile. "But if you see that sinful Ede rush right back to your safe sister!"

Ella laughed.

After she delivered the pastry to Clara, Ella went about the marketing. First some sweet paprika. The table at the spice seller's was crowded with little bags, each containing a different spice, the aromas mixing chaotically. Mother wanted a specific paprika, which the seller had. Placing the little parcel in her shopping basket, Ella moved on to the tents selling potatoes.

She wondered about Ede. Did all men want sex before marriage? Certainly he did. Was Clara right? Did that make him a bad man? Maybe it did. Maybe Mother was right to forbid her seeing him. But no. If it was truly sinful would he tell her? Yes, he would tell her. He didn't believe in sin. No, that wasn't true. He did believe in sin, just, he didn't think that this was a sin.

Or something.

She wasn't sure.

She stopped at Mother's favorite potato merchant. They had sold out, so she had to find another vendor. She walked along the aisle of tents, stopping at each one that had potatoes, looking at the vegetables.

Did Ede believe that lust was sinful? He believed it was shameful, he had said so himself. Or maybe lust was not shameful, it was his visit with the lady of the night that was shameful.

She had to admire him, for telling her. She had to trust him, because he had opened his heart to her. He didn't have to. But he said he felt he had to. It was a brave thing to do.

She did trust him.

She did admire him.

Ella found potatoes that looked good and bargained with the farmer. She was not good at bargaining, at least that was what Cook said. But this time, she thought she had done a good job, and she let several coins drop into her pocket as a reward to herself. Mother would certainly scold her when she quoted a price higher than she actually paid, but how could she find out?

Besides, Ella thought it was only fair. Miklos got pocket money, but Father didn't think girls needed to have money. So she took a little when she went shopping. She never spent any, since Mother or Father would notice that she had something they hadn't provided. But at least she had the money. By now she had a little fortune, or so it seemed.

Now for the meat.

Ella hated the old meat vendor. He always called her My Little Sunshine and snickered, wiping his hands on his blood stained apron.

She found his tent, pleased that the old man was not there. In his stead, his son, a boy a little younger than she was, waited on customers.

"My Little Sunshine, what would you need?"

Ella stared at him. At least he didn't snicker. No he had a warm smile.

She made a quick decision and struck a good bargain. Maybe she should be easier on the young fellow. Maybe his father would be angry with him, angry he had not charged more. But maybe the boy got pocket money.

She let a few coins slide into her pocket and put the rest of the change in the leather purse. The young merchant wrapped the meat in paper and handed the bundle to her.

Mother had said she could get some berries if she found some nice ones. Ella walked along the stalls to where the poorer peasants sold their produce. They sat on the ground or on little benches, their plums and apricots, blueberries and peaches set in large baskets on the ground.

She walked to her favorite vendor, an old Croat woman. She liked buying from this old crone, not only because she had extraordinary fruit, but because it gave Ella a chance to practice her Croat.

Ella didn't have many words, but the old woman always helped her with the names of the produce and giggled as Ella tried to remember words.

Today she had raspberries, which Ella tasted. The burst of acid sweet filled her mouth as she bit down on the fruit. She bought a small bag, paying more for it than she probably should. Part of the price, Ella thought, paid for her Croat lesson.

Her shopping done, Ella returned to the bench where Clara sat waiting for her.

"You took forever!"

"Yes, well I had to search for potatoes. But now I'm here."

Clara pushed herself off the bench and started to head toward home.

"Do you think Maid really would steal napkins if Mother didn't lock the cabinets?"

Ella was happy that Clara was onto something other than sex and Ede.

"I don't know. Maybe, if she were poor enough."

"But Mother says she doesn't need anything, since she lives with us and eats with us. So she isn't really poor."

"Maybe she would like to buy something. A pretty blouse? To wear to church?"

"Maybe."

"Or maybe she has a poor mother that needs money."

"Oh. Maybe. Then Mother should give her money and then she wouldn't steal."

"Mother always feels short of money."

Ella thought of all the times Mother had complained, about the cost of food, of how much the dress maker charged, the need for new curtains. It seemed something new was always needed and Mother never had enough money.

"Why do you ask about Maid?"

"She just seems so nice and Mother is so mean to her. She has to ask Mother for clean linens when she changes the beds. Then Mother unlocks the closet, pulls out the clean linens and counts what is still in the closet. And Maid, she looks so worried when Mother counts. Mother counts slowly. One. Two. Three. As if they will never get to the end of the counting."

Ella had seen Mother do this a thousand times: Mother selecting a key from the chatelaine that hung at her waist, fitting the key into the lock, turning the key slowly, because the lock was untrustworthy? Or maybe Mother enjoyed prolonging the ritual, an accusatory sequence. She had keys for the linen closet, for the closet with the silver serving plates, another for the silver utensils. And of course she had a key for the little drawer in the pantry where she kept the household money. Just this morning, Ella stood, biting her lip, while Mother, fat, gray, angry Mother went through the ritual of getting money for the marketing. It was as if Mother wanted to fight.

Therese Returns

The next day, Ella was reading in her room when Therese returned from the herbalist. Her eyes were red, but the rest of her face was blue-white.

"Are you all right?"

"Yes, yes." Therese dropped her satchel on the floor and sank onto her bed. "I just need to rest a moment, then I'll be fine."

Ella watched as the slight figure leaned to one side and then collapsed onto the coverlet.

"Therese?"

There was no response.

"Therese, are you OK?"

Silence.

Ella got a cloth from the washstand, dipped it into the bowl, squeezed out the excess water, and mopped it across the ashen face. Therese's breath came in little wisps and she cried out in French.

Ella leaned closer. "Therese? What did you say?"

Therese turned her head toward the wall. As Ella leaned over Therese, still trying to soothe her, she felt warm moisture on her hand.

She looked down.

She screamed.

A red pool of blood had spread across the white bed cover.

Jumping up, Ella raced to find Mother, who was in the kitchen counting out the silver for supper that evening.

"Mother, please come."

"Wait until I have finished here."

"Mother, please!"

Her mother looked up and studied her daughter.

"Very well. Cook, we will place everything back and start again when I return."

She replaced the utensils in the cabinet and found the proper key on her chatelaine.

How could this take so long? "Mother, Therese is sick. Very sick."

"We must have order in this house. I have interrupted my work already."

Mother wiggled the key, side to side, to get it into the keyhole and carefully turned it. Again she pushed the key side to side to get it to slide out. She stood, smoothing her skirt and walked toward the girls' room.

"What seems to be the matter?"

Ella trailed behind her mother. "She didn't feel well this morning, so she went to the herbalist."

Mother stopped, turned, and looked at her daughter. "The herbalist?"

Ella bit her lip. Maybe she shouldn't....

Mother, quickening her pace, seemed to understand everything. Looking over her shoulder, her voice loud and commanding, she said. "Go to Father's study, close the door, and stay there until I come for you."

Ella loved Father's study. He took pride in Ella's ability to read Hungarian, German, French, even Latin and English, so he had granted her the privilege of using his study and reading his books whenever he was not there.

Mother, seeming to know what pleased Ella, usually forbade her going there.

The sweet smell of Father's pipe smoke greeted her as she

carefully opened the door. Her eyes caressed the dark wood of the bookcase, filled with what she considered her books, because, really, Father never read them and neither did Miklos and certainly not Mother. Ella had taught Clara to read, just as Ede had taught her, and Clara liked to read. But she liked to be read to even more.

Ella opened the left-most of the bookcase's four doors and pulled out the Bible. It was a Latin Bible. Why the Bible? She wasn't sure. She was just drawn to it and she opened it to the most worn pages, *The Song of Songs*:

> *Let him kiss me with the kisses of his mouth--*
> *for your love is more delightful than wine.*
> *Pleasing is the fragrance of your perfumes;*
> *your name is like perfume poured out.*
> *No wonder the young women love you!*
> *Take me away with you--let us hurry!*
> *Let the king bring me into his chambers.*

The wall clock rang the hour. She loved the clock sounds in Father's study, the chimes, and the mellow beat of the gold pendulum, as if it were the heart of the room, and as long as it marked the seconds with its beat and the hours with its chime, all was well. She focused on its slender hands.

It was late.

Mother was taking forever with Therese.

Was Therese OK?

Somehow she had ceased to worry when Mother took charge of the situation, but now, now that it had been more than an hour, she wondered what was wrong.

She wondered whether she dared leave the room, which Mother had forbidden. To consider her options, she laid the book on the table and went around Father's desk to the topmost right-hand drawer, Father's candy drawer. He always kept his smoking supplies there – matches, pipes, cleaners – and a supply of the hard mint candy he liked to give out.

Ella had discovered that one day when Father had refilled his pockets from the supply in the drawer. From then on, when she was in the office alone, she would take one, for now, and two more, as reserves in case of being sent to her room without dinner, Mother's favorite punishment. Her secret supply of Father's candies had come in handy quite often. She opened the drawer, slid two into her pocket and was about to take another for now when the door creaked.

She could see Mother's silhouette standing tall, her fists on her hips.

Mother Understands

"Is Therese going to be OK?" Ella came around from the desk, pushing the drawer closed with her hip.

"I wouldn't be worrying about that hussy."

Her mother's chuckle had no humor. As she moved into the room, Ella could see her face. Her cheeks red, her lips pressed down in a frown.

"You won't be seeing more of her."

"What happened?"

"Never mind." She rounded behind Ella pushing her toward the door. "To your room. Now."

Ella tried to look at Mother over her shoulder, but received a non-too-gentle shove.

"No dawdling."

Ella walked down the hall, up the stairs, and into her room.

Mother followed her into the room and stood, blocking the door with her ample figure. "Sit."

Ella sank down into a chair, staring at her mother.

"So, I cannot trust you to follow any of my orders."

Ella stared. What had happened to Therese?

"I tell you to stay in your room, and you go into the kitchen. I forbid dinner and you eat anyway."

She held up her fist, as if she would slam it into Ella. "And then, most important," She shook her fist. "I tell you not to see Ede, and you find a way to see him."

Ella kept her eyes locked on Mother's.

"What do you have to say?"

Ella straightened her spine. "Yes. Yes, I did."

"You admit it, you brazen hussy."

"Yes, I did." She was tempted to say 'and I saw him alone' knowing that would upset her mother even more, but she didn't know what happened to Therese. She didn't want to get her in more trouble.

"And you saw him alone."

Mother already knew! Good! "Yes, I did."

"You idiot!"

Mother sighed, unclenched her fist and put her hand over her mouth. She dropped her hand and stared at her daughter.

"Do you think we will ever be able to find a husband for you if the town knows you see men alone?"

So that was the trouble. Mother was afraid of gossip. "I don't want a husband!" But she had said yes to Ede. Well, Mother didn't need to know that.

"That's what you think. You're as much a hussy as your friend Therese."

Therese was not her friend, she was Mother's employee.

"I cannot control you."

Ella looked her mother in the eye.

"I cannot trust you to stay in your room by telling you to do so. So I will lock you in this room."

Ella sat, her hands in her lap, her eyes on her mother's.

"Cook will bring you your meals."

Ella stared.

"Maid will tidy up."

Ella's situation had become clear. She was imprisoned.

"I will unlock the door for them. I will wait while they are here. I will relock the door when they leave."

Ella wondered how long this incarceration would last.

"Father and I have to decide what to do about you."

She would be here for a while.

She wondered what Father would say. She thought of him as her ally. He was proud of her, proud that she could speak and read and write so many languages, proud that she could do math in her head, proud that she was, as he said, his little beauty. He would find a way out of this.

"Until we decide, I will make sure you do not leave the room." Mother's skirts swished as she turned and left, pulling the door shut behind her.

Ella could hear her put the key in the lock, wiggling it from side to side. She heard the bolt engage as the key turned, heard the key jiggle as it was removed.

Ella Considers Her Situation

Ella stood by the window. She could open it and escape, but the room was on the third floor. Maybe she could use her bed sheets to lower herself to the ground, like Huck Finn. That made her smile. She had Huck here to keep her company, and *A Tale of Two Cities*. She would not be lonely or bored.

She looked over at her bed. The linens from one bed would not be long enough to lower herself to the ground. She could tie her linens with Therese's. She looked at the other bed. An uneven stain, the size of a serving platter, spread across the white cover, the middle bright red, the edges drying to a brown. She didn't want to touch that.

She turned her back, looking out the window. Dusk was settling over Fő út.

On nice evenings, such as tonight, young men would line either side of the broad road and young women, the maids and the cooks, the waitresses and the washerwomen, would walk up and down smiling at the men. This evening's parade was in progress.

Some couples formed, the man wrapping his arm around the young woman's waist. These women didn't need matchmakers. They found their own mates.

Maybe it would be better to be one of these women.

Not ladies.

Just women.

If she were to escape from the window, she would have to find a time when the street was deserted. She hadn't really paid attention to the street until now. Maybe the street would never be deserted. Then she would have to find another way out. But tonight she would keep watch, she would find out if Fő út was ever empty.

It cheered her, having a plan, a goal: escape!

But what would she do once she escaped? She wasn't sure. Find Ede? She could go to his house and see if he were there. Would he know that she was "in jail"? On the wedding day he was able to find out. Maybe Clara would tell him. Or Miklos?

What was Miklos thinking? Was he upset that Therese was gone.

Was Therese gone? Ella assumed that she had been let go. How would Miklos feel?

Probably he wouldn't care.

She was drowning in fatigue. She lay down on her bed.

Ella woke to the sound of banging. She sat up, confused, the room dark, the lamps not lit.

"Open up!" Miklos's voice rasped. "Open up now!"

She got up and tried to open the door, but it was locked. Her memories of the last hours, Mother's anger, her imprisonment flooded her mind.

"Shh!" Maybe Miklos could help her escape, but she didn't want him to wake the house. "Mother has locked me in. I can't open the door."

She heard jangling, a key slipping easily into the lock and turning, the bolt dropping open. The door flew open to Miklos holding a lamp, his eyes wide, scanning the room. "Where's Therese?"

"Gone."

"Gone?"

"Yes. She was ill...."

Miklos rushed to Therese's bed. His hand hovered above the

bloody stain. "What's this…?"

"And I told Mother."

Miklos turned toward his sister, his lips trembling. "You told Mother? You fool!"

Ella backed away. "Therese was ill. She was very ill and I didn't know what to do."

"You idiot." He turned from her and went to the window. "She had an abortion. Of course she was ill."

"An abortion?"

"When did she leave?"

"What's an abortion?"

He looked at her, his face twisted with a nasty smile. "You don't know what an abortion is, Virgin Mary?"

"What is it?" She glared at him.

"I've no time to educate you now. When did she leave?"

"Oh, Miklos, I don't know. Mother came, told me to go to Father's study, and when she finally got me, maybe an hour or so later – the clock only chimed once – she said I would never see Therese again, called her a hussy."

Miklos pulled the drawer to Therese's bed cabinet open and riffled through the contents, stuffing several papers in his pocket. He straightened and headed to the door.

"Where are you going?"

Without looking at her, he said, "To find Therese."

He was gone.

And the door was open.

She could leave. But where would she go?

And how was it that Miklos had keys?

Maybe she should leave now, while the door was open. She grasped a strand of her hair and slid it between her fingers.

Abortion? She could go to Father's study and look it up in the dictionary.

She looked over at Therese's empty bed, the bed with the stain, the stain, which had grown darker.

An abortion must be serious. Mother had sent her to her room many times, but she had never, ever locked her in before. If she went to Father's study she might run into Mother. She had seen Mother angry often, but today she shook, her voice snarled with fury.

Better not to provoke her further.

Abortion.

She could figure this out. Abortion sounded like the Latin noun abortionem. The verb would be aboriri. Ab would be away from, down, off. Oriri would be rise, get up. appear, become visible, come to exist, originate, born. Away from exist. Away from originate. Away from born. Away from born, away from born....

Was Therese pregnant?

Ella opened Therese's drawer and looked through the contents. A few scraps of paper, a pen, a battered Bible, a letter. A letter! A letter in French, from some woman. A friend perhaps.

Ella began to read:

"Here it is very bad. We have little to eat. Do not think to come here with mouths to feed." Maybe Therese had written to ask for help? Mouths to feed? Not a mouth, but mouths. Plural mouths. Would that be Therese? And a baby?

She turned back to the letter. "Would the church help? Or your man? Would he marry you? Or pay for a..." and here was a word she did not know: 'avortement.'

Like the English avoid?

"The church says it is a sin. But the church does not have to feed and clothe it."

What sin was that?

"I have had several. Not fun. But better than a baby."

Yes, Therese was pregnant!

"You bleed. You feel sick, like a bad period, like giving birth. But not so bad."

Ella dropped the letter and looked over at Therese's bed. That was it. Therese was pregnant and she did something to get rid of the pregnancy. And she came home and bled. Mother knew exactly what was going on. That was why she called her a hussy. And she must have told Mother about Ella's meetings with Ede.

It all made sense.

She smiled.

It all made sense.

Her eyes scanned the bed and the stain. It made terrible sense. She put her hand over her mouth. It made terrible, terrible sense.

Poor Therese! Mother had let her go, for sure. And where would she go? She had written to her friend – or was it her sister – who didn't want her. Could she go to the church? Probably. That would be what Ella would do if she were Therese.

Or maybe she would marry Miklos, if Father would allow it.

She could not imagine marrying Miklos. Sarcastic, caustic Miklos.

But maybe that would be better than the church.

Ella's eyes wandered back to the open door.

She could leave right now. Where would she go if she were to run away? Not to the church. She was not pregnant! No, she would go to Ede. Ede with his sweet, sweet kisses. She would marry him and they would be happy together. Maybe even Mother and Father would be happy. Ede could support a family. He could marry. He had said so. It would be perfect.

They would marry and move to Budapest, far away from Mother. They would live together and work together and they would kiss and....

She thought of the horses. The mare stretched her neck, her head a little low.

Yes, they would kiss and they would make love. Did the mare like the stallion on her? She didn't seem to object. Maybe it would be nice. Ede said it was nice, said they could avoid having children.

Ella stopped pacing.

Avoid having children?

Like abortion?

Was that what he meant?

No.

She would not 'avortement' having children.

That would not happen.

She closed the door.

Miklos Brings News

Ella felt a breath on her cheek. She opened her eyes and looked up into Miklos' troubled face. "What's wrong?"

Miklos placed his oil lamp on the bed cabinet. "I found her."

She sat up. "Therese?"

"Yes, yes. Therese."

"Is she all right?"

"No. Not unless you believe she's going to heaven."

Ella pulled her covers around her. "She is...."

"Yes, she's dead."

"What...?"

"I went to our place, our place in the forest...." He walked over to the window and looked out at the gloom.

"I told her to meet me there if we needed to...." He rubbed his arm across his eyes. "Well, if things didn't go well with the...." He swiveled around. "If they didn't go well with the abortion...."

He recrossed the room and sank to Therese's bed. "I should never have gone on that wild goose chase. Father told me to go to Nagyrécse. To a customer. To pick up something they did not like and give them a replacement. He said it was most important to go, right then."

Miklos slammed his fist into the bed. "He insisted I had to go."

Ella had never seen Miklos so defenseless, his sneering confidence gone.

"Of course, the man in Nagyrécse knew nothing about the

replacement." He raised his fist again and forced it into the mattress. "It was a ruse, a way to take me away when Therese needed me. It was Mother's idea to get me out of the way when Therese needed me."

This rambling didn't make sense to Ella, but she said nothing.

In the light of Miklos' lamp Ella saw dark blotches on his pants, on his shirt, on his face and his hands.

"She's dead, Ella. Dead." A tear glistened on his cheek. "She was there. Waiting for me. In a pool of blood."

He put hands over his face.

Ella did not know what to say. "I'm sorry."

The room was silent but for his soft sobs.

"You must have loved her." Ella never thought Miklos could love, but maybe he could.

Miklos let his hands drop. "I love her. Yes! I love her!" He shook his head, again drawing his arm across his eyes. "I loved her."

"I'm sorry." Ella sat next to him and wrapped her arms around him. "So sorry."

He embraced her and held her close, his breast heaving with each sob, his warm tears spilling onto her shoulder.

His cries increased so that Ella feared he would wake their parents. Too bad, she thought. If they woke and found them, what crime had they committed? They were mourning the death of a... What would Ella call Therese? Not a friend, but, well, never mind. They were mourning the death of Miklos' love. That was enough. And if Mother could not understand, if it sent her into another spasm of fury, Ella didn't care.

She rocked Miklos to and fro, as she had rocked Clara when she had cried over her childish tragedies. But this was an adult tragedy, not a broken toy or a skinned knee.

Miklos' cries were softer now, his body relaxed. He exhaled a shuddered breath, sat up, withdrew a handkerchief from his pocket and wiped his face.

"Thank you, Sister."

Sister? She could not remember him calling her sister. It was so formal. But not unkind.

Ella pulled away from him. Somehow what had seemed natural before now felt awkward. "I'm sorry."

"Thank you." He stood, straightening his clothes, noticing the stains on his hands. Looking further he saw the blood on his clothes. He started to the door.

"You better lock the door when you leave," Ella said. "You don't want Mother to know you have been here, that you have keys...."

"I don't care what Mother knows. She killed Therese. She can go to hell."

Mother's Plans

"Morning, Miss."

Cook placed a tray holding coffee, rolls and jam on Ella's table. She seemed not to see the blood stains, not just on Therese's bed but now also on Ella's night dress.

Mother stood at the door watching all, saying nothing. When she left, she did not lock the door. Ella could only guess what had happened.

Maid came in later, bringing fresh linens. Again Mother stood at the door. Maid said nothing as she changed the beds and tidied up.

When Maid and Mother left, Ella settled at her table, Huck Finn before her, trying to read. Her eyes followed the words, each word clear, but she was unable to concentrate enough to put them together into a sentence.

Pictures of Therese on her bed, the red blotch growing beside her, intruded. The feeling of Miklos' stiff body heaving with cries would not allow her to think.

Finally she closed the book and took up her knitting. The rhythm of her work calmed her: pierce fabric, twine yarn, pull through, pierce fabric, twine yarn, pull through. It was unthinking work that allowed yesterday's images to dart here and there, not calming her, but making it bearable.

Miklos brought her dinner.

Miklos alone.

Mother did not follow.

"Thank you, Sister."

Sister rang in her ears again, strange but welcome.

Miklos placed the tray on the table and sat down in the other chair.

"You were kind last night."

She stared at her brother, a different brother, a kind and considerate brother. Maybe this was the Miklos Therese loved.

"You're welcome."

She brought a spoonful of stew to her lips. It was too hot.

"Are you all right?"

She blew on the stew and looked at him.

"Yes, yes." He smiled, a kind smile, not a sarcastic smile. "I am all right."

"What happened with Mother? She isn't locking me in anymore."

"I told her that I had keys, that I could unlock the door anytime I wanted."

"You did?"

She took a bite of the meat. It tasted off. She placed the spoon back in the bowl.

"What did she say?"

He looked away. "She just sputtered."

Miklos' sarcastic grin spread across his face. "She can't do much to me. Father needs me. He won't let Mother get in the way."

Ella considered Miklos' statement. He had power where she had none. She picked up a roll and bit into it.

Miklos's face relaxed into a kinder look."They sent Clara off to Grandmother's."

Ella nodded. Of course they did. They didn't want Clara to know what was happening. But she would figure it out. She was a clever little thing.

He leaned back and reached into his pocket. "I brought you a little present."

She looked up. "A present?"

"Yes." He held up a fob with a dozen keys. "Your very own set."

"Oh!"

"Let me explain what they are." He rattled them off: this to the china cabinet, this to the silver drawer, and on and on.

"I don't think I can remember all of them."

"It doesn't matter. If you want to open something, just try them until you find the right one. In general the small keys are to drawers and cabinets, the large ones are to doors."

She nodded, putting the bread back on the tray and taking the fob, looking at each key.

She looked up at him. "Does Mother know I have these?"

"No."

She nodded.

"And I have some other news for you."

"Other news?"

"Mrs. Farkas was here."

Mrs. Farkas, the matchmaker, the fox-like matchmaker.

Miklos stared at her. "And Mother Mary Theresa."

Ella exhaled, her body sagging. "So if they can't marry me off, they will send me to a convent?"

Miklos nodded.

She had a secret weapon. Ede.

But why hadn't he spoken to Father yet?

Ella's Plans

The next morning, Ella stood at the window looking out, her hand in her pocket, fingering the keys. The bright sun promised another hot, sticky day.

She would have to leave. Ede had not asked Father. But why?

Did he change his mind? Had Father refused him? Or maybe Mother had put up some objection. She didn't know. But she couldn't stay and let Mother decide her fate. She had to leave.

She wouldn't marry some old man that Mother thought appropriate. She thought of the bachelors Zsuzsi had mentioned, repulsive old men.

And she wouldn't go into a convent, even if that would be better than marrying Mother's choice.

She had a little time to think through her plans. Weddings did not happen overnight.

But maybe being sent to a convent did?

She didn't know. She couldn't think of anyone who was whisked away to a nunnery. Her cousin Irma was in a convent, but she was at least 15 years older than Ella and Ella couldn't remember when she had gone or why.

She thought of Irma's rough red hands.

She had better escape now.

Would she go to Ede? Even if Father or Mother had refused him, maybe he would still run away with her.

No. She didn't want to be in his debt.

He said he wanted to marry.

If he did he could follow her.

He was going to Budapest. That was the obvious thing to do, go to Budapest.

Would Ede find her in Budapest?

He was smart. He would find her.

Or maybe she should tell Miklos of her plans?

Miklos. She didn't know what to make of Miklos.

Her fingers slid over the cool metal of the keys. She was happy to have his gift. But did she trust him? Maybe he was happy to have her gone.

No.

She was being unkind.

Or maybe she should tell Ede.

But how?

If Clara were here, she could carry a message.

But Clara had been sent to Grandmother's, until the tempest passed, she guessed. Maybe Clara would have a good time at Grandmother's. Maybe she would see a stallion mount a mare.

Stop it.

No time for bitterness.

Think.

How could she tell Ede? Miklos was the only route. She didn't trust Miklos.

No that was an excuse.

She didn't want to tell Ede. She wasn't sure of Ede. His kisses were sweet, but something inside, some instinct told her she must do this by herself.

She thought of the abortion, the image of Therese on her bed, the red stain spreading.

She would leave by herself. She would go to Budapest. Ede could find her there, if he truly wanted to.

How would she get to Budapest?

She would take the train! No problem. A train ran from Nagykanizsa to Budapest.

But what would the stationmaster say. "Why, Miss Weisel, going to Budapest alone?"

She could see his brow wrinkled in the question, his eyes sparkling with malicious light.

She would have to have a good answer. He must know about Therese's death. All Nagykanizsa knew by now.

"Yes, yes. My Aunt Ilona has been unwell and asked that we come to her. But Mother is ill."

She could let that dangle. Mr. Stationmaster would assume it was the distress of Therese's death that caused Mother to be "ill."

But then why would Ella not stay with Mother?

Good question.

That should confuse Mr. Stationmaster. He wouldn't ask more questions.

Aunt Ilona, Mother's older sister, did live in Budapest, but Ella had no intention of seeing her. Still, in case Mr. Stationmaster knew of Aunt Ilona, this would make her story sound true.

And it would mislead her parents if they tried to find her.

So, hopefully, she had stopped Mr. Stationmaster's questions.

She would ask for a ticket to Budapest.

She probably should buy a round-trip ticket. Ella wasn't sure. She could say she only needed a one-way ticket, that she wasn't sure how she would return. Maybe Aunt Ilona would come back with her and she wasn't sure how they would come or by what route. She needn't tell the stationmaster this, only if he asked why she wanted a one-way ticket.

So she would buy a one-way ticket to Budapest.

How much would it cost?

She had no idea.

Where would she stay once she got to Budapest?

Blank.

Maybe she would go to the church and ask to stay there until she could find a job? Would that lead to a convent?

She sighed. She must not go to the church.

She must find a job. What kind of job could she find?

She knew what she wanted. She wanted to be a translator. But how could she manage that?

Blank.

So many things she did not know.

Maybe it didn't matter. Maybe she could figure this out once she was in Budapest. The important thing was to get to Budapest. She would take the train. She would need to pay for the ticket. She didn't know how much it would cost.

She smiled. She knew the price of a pork roast or a few grams of paprika or a kilo of potatoes. But she had no idea how much a train ticket to Budapest cost.

Could she find out? She must plan this, so she was not throwing money at the stationmaster. That would look suspicious. How could she find that out?

Miklos would know, but did she dare ask him, let him know her plans? She would have to, unless she could find a better way.

And even if she did know how much it would be, how would she pay for it?

She thought of the pile of coins she had skimmed off her shopping at the market. But surely that would not be enough. And she couldn't pay for the ticket with a pile of change, even if she had enough. That would look suspicious too.

This plan of hers was not working. She wrapped her arms

around herself and stared out the window.

Father to the Rescue

It was late afternoon when Father entered Ella's room, his step lighter than usual.

"Hello, my princess." He smiled, his eyes sparkling. "I have wonderful news for you!"

"Oh." It had happened so quickly? She doubted Father would be so pleased if she was to be sent to a convent. Or would he? Surely he didn't think Ella, his rebellious daughter, would be happy in a convent. No. It must be a husband. The only question was who.

Father's eyes skimmed her face. "Cheer up, my little Ella. It is very good news." He patted her on the back as he sat beside her on her bed, placing his walking stick beside him. "News you will like."

She folded her hands on her lap. She refused to give him the satisfaction that she wished to know her future.

In fact, he did not know her future. She would run away. She had already decided that. So it really didn't matter who they'd found to marry her.

She looked at her hands, rubbing one thumb over the other.

"Ede."

Her eyes darted to Father's face. "Oh."

"Yes, isn't it marvelous? Wonderful?" He rubbed her back as he spoke, his words cascading out. "Mother isn't happy about this. Of course I should not tell you that. She doesn't like Ede, especially after she found out that the two of you...." He beamed at his daughter. "Well, no need to go into that."

Having caught his breath, Father continued. "Anyhow, he came to me early in the morning. The morning after... well... we don't need to talk about that either. Early in the morning. I'd hardly finished my breakfast. He came to me all pale and agitated."

Father's smile widened, his eyes twinkled. "Like someone in love!" His smile grew even broader. "He loves you, my dear."

She nodded.

He grasped his walking stick, running his fingers over the design embossed in the silver handle.

"Not that love should have anything to do with this. Marriage is a business arrangement. And, like an idiot, Ede had not thought through the details, had not discussed this with his brother."

"His brother?" Ella would have understood having to discuss it with his father, but why his brother?

"Yes, yes, my darling. Endre and Ede officially own the construction company together, so Endre had to be consulted."

He tapped the tip of his cane on the floor. "But those are details you needn't worry about."

He stood and stretched. "Anyway, Ede said he wanted to marry you because he loves you."

Father sat again, and snorted a chuckle. "Mother holds this against him, of course. She says he has no sense. I suppose she is right."

He shrugged. "But he loves you and that melted my heart."

Father's fingers returned to tracing the design on the cane's silver handle. "He said Miklos had come to him. Told him about... well the whole story... and he had come to me as quickly as he could and made his proposition."

He shook his head. "Mother says he is too young. But I have always liked the boy."

Sighing, Father placed the cane beside him. "Smart boy, in some ways. School learning. Maybe not such good business sense."

He looked at Ella. "Nice family. His father was my friend." His lip compressed, a cloud saddened his gaze. "I miss him."

Father sighed and placed his arm around Ella's shoulder. "You look pale, my little one."

He pulled her close so that her head rested on his shoulder. "I thought this would please you, but you're so quiet."

She shuddered. Ede had talked to Father. But why had it taken so long for Father to agree? She felt numb.

"It's been... difficult... with Therese...."

"Oh yes. That. Yes. Things have been... well, complicated. Yes. Very complicated."

He rubbed her back. Ella wondered whether this was to comfort her or whether it was to ease his concerns.

"So Ede comes to me with this, well, not really a proposal, this declaration of love. So what did I do?" He looked at her.

She shook her head, waiting for his answer.

"What any reasonable businessman would do. I went to see Endre."

Father sighed.

"Lucky Endre was here. He spends so much time at his projects and his projects are always out of town. But I guess he has taken a little time off since he just married and I guess the newlyweds are... well, having some time together. So Endre was home."

Ella nodded. She really didn't know Endre, Ede's brother. She had hardly ever spoken to him. Father had done business with Tódor, the boys' father for years, Tódor using Father's iron works in his buildings. Father might be happy simply because this match would cement his relationship to Endre from one of business to one of family.

Father chuckled. "I know, I know. Marriage is usually an agreement between families, with the families not really talking to each other. They talk to the matchmaker."

He nodded to himself.

"But there is not much that is usual about this. You are young. Not that young, but young. He is young, very young, just starting out in life. He'll be a lawyer. That's OK."

Father tilted his head to the side as he grimaced. Clearly he was not sure it was OK.

"It would have been better if he were a businessman. But, well, you don't need to know about that."

Father pulled mints from his pocket and offered one to Ella. She shook her head. He unwrapped a candy and put it in his mouth.

"And Mother was sure that we had to find you a match right now, because, well, because of everything, she just thought it was best to...."

Ella had to smile. Sometimes Father was graceless. But he was kind.

Too bad he married Mother. Did he think his marriage had been a good business arrangement? It didn't seem to have anything to do with love.

Father turned his gaze to his daughter. "And I thought you would be pleased. Because the two of you, well, you have been friends since...."

"Since before I can remember." Indeed, Ede had always been a part of her life.

"So you are pleased!" He nodded and grinned.

She tried to put on a happy face, but the numbness persisted. Best to play to Father's hopes.

"Yes."

She put her hand in her pocket and felt the coolness of the keys.

"Yes. Ede is my friend."

"Good. You are happy. I mean a marriage is a business arrangement, but it would be better if you were happy. And you are, so give your father a good hug."

She slid her arm around his waist and leaned against his shoulder. She inhaled his scent of pipe tobacco and mint candy, the smell of Father, sweet and pungent... comforting.

"So Endre and I have it all figured out. Mother is in a tizzy, of course. I'm sure she will be here in no time to fuss about all the things women fuss about when there is a, well, a wedding."

A wedding did not happen overnight. There would be dresses and invitations and visits from the priest.

But none of that mattered. Only one thing must happen: she needed to talk to Ede.

"Father, may I see Ede now? I mean, since we are to be married."

"Of course, my little dove. Let me talk to Mother."

The Necklace

Ede and Ella sat under "their" tree in the woods. Now that they were engaged, Mother didn't object to their being seen in public together. They had walked to the park, his hand on her elbow, talking of nothing: the warm weather, a bluebird on a branch and the nest, now deserted, next to the bird. As they settled under the tree, it seemed more inviting than any other place in Nagykanizsa.

She drew her knees up to her chest. He sat straight, looking at her.

"I'm sorry it took so long to get everybody to agree to the marriage." He snorted. "This idea, that the agreement was really between our families rather than between us, it's just medieval!"

She smiled. Smiled because he, too, thought the concept of marriage as a business arrangement was wrong.

"But I think it is important to keep everyone happy." His eyes sparkled as he looked at her. "I think everyone is happy." This was a question really.

She wasn't happy. She was confused. But she nodded. Better to let him have his say and then they could talk.

"Miklos came to me, in a state. Poor fellow." Ede expelled a breath, his body sagging. "But that is for another time...." He closed his eyes, shaking his read. "And poor Therese!"

"I have a question." Ella swallowed. "It's about Therese. About what happened to Therese."

He looked up at her, his face somber.

"Yes?

"I mean the...." She pulled a strand of hair from her bun and rolled it between her fingers. "I mean the abortion."

"Yes." He squinted. "The abortion."

"That's what you call it when you are pregnant and you get rid of the baby?"

"Yes."

"Is that what you meant?" She held her breath, so her words came in a raspy whisper. "Is that how one prevents having children?"

He smiled. Then he laughed, his smooth rich laugh.

"No, my little Kis Maria." He shook his head. "No, no, no!"

She interrupted, her voice loud and rough. "Don't laugh at me."

His smile faded, replaced by a serious look, but soft and warm.

"No, my beloved Ella. There are other ways, ways that do not hurt, that you will hardly notice."

She nodded. "I don't want children."

"Yes, we have agreed on that." He scrunched his face. "But why?"

"Because... look at Mother. All she does is care for children and the house. I don't want to be a slave like that."

"OK. But with enough help...."

"Mother has Cook and Maid, Moni, and even a companion for me. How much more help can one have?"

"OK." He sighed. "We can't figure all these things out, Ella, not in this moment. Things will change. We will have to talk and discuss and argue."

She inhaled. "Yes. We shall argue. We shall argue a lot."

He kissed her forehead, her cheek, her mouth. He held her at arm's length, his eyes wet.

"My Ella. My Beloved Ella."

His hands on her cheeks, he pulled her toward him and kissed her again. And again.

"We need to get back." She tried to tidy her hair. "Mother has relaxed a bit, but there are limits."

"Are there?" His laugh drifted through the forest.

"Shhh."

"What?" His merry eyes sparkled. "Are you such a proper young lady?"

She swatted him. His hand grabbed her arm and pulled her toward him. "Just one more kiss."

He took more than one, but finally stood, dusting himself off, then gave her a hand up.

"I've got a little something for my wife."

"Wife?"

"Ella, as far as I am concerned, we are now married. All we needed was our mutual consent."

"OK." She grinned at him. "But I think Mother is going to insist on the church ceremony and the state will insist we see a judge."

"And we will do all that, just to keep Mother and the state happy. But now you are my wife. And I have something for my wife."

He took a small black leather box from his jacket pocket. Opening the box, he pulled out a heart-shaped locket. A deep green emerald gleamed from the center; sparkling diamonds surrounded the green gem and arched gracefully to the locket's rim. Black enamel edged the lines of diamonds, setting off their dazzle.

Ella had never thought she cared for jewelry, but this was beautiful. It was beautiful and it was a gift from her husband.

She looked into his hazel eyes. His broad smile revealed a

dimple in his right cheek. That felt strange, that she had a husband.

"Thank you, my husband."

And it sounded strange.

He fastened the necklace around her neck, turned her toward him and studied her.

"Just as I thought. It is the same color as your eyes. The day I decided I wanted to marry you, I bought it, knowing that the emerald was the same color as your eyes."

He took her hand and they started toward home.

"Maybe our children will have such beautiful eyes."

Getting the Trousseau in Order

Immediately after breakfast the next day, Mother bustled into Ella's room, pen, ink bottle, and paper in hand. Her skirt swished as she settled in a chair at the table.

"We must sort through your trousseau and see what we still need." She flattened the paper on the table. "So I can tell Father what we must buy. How much money we will need."

Ella cringed inwardly, but remembered Ede's words: "We will do these things to keep Mother happy."

"Yes Mother. Thank you."

"My, you have become such a good daughter. Maybe we should have married you off sooner."

Ella tried to smile at this, but the statement had a nasty tone. She looked at Mother, whose smile seemed forced.

"I will write things down as you take them out of the trunk. And we will have to sort through the things in your cabinet too."

Mother had a special cabinet for her daughters' crystal and china, separate shelves for Ella and Clara.

Mother held her pen ready to write.

"When we are finished we will list what we still need."

Ella nodded. "Of course."

She opened the trunk.

Mother had enjoyed looking through things, each time she added to the collection. Ella had hated these times.

Zsuzsi had wanted to see what she had, but Ella had refused to show her, but not because she was ashamed of her trousseau. Indeed, sometimes she wondered whether Zsuzsi might be envious of the things in the trunk.

It was something else. Ella didn't want to think of the trousseau and what it represented: a proper Hungarian marriage. She didn't want to be a proper Hungarian wife. She wanted something else.

But Ede had promised her that something else, that project – it sounded like a crusade – to help Hungary. Going through the trousseau was just a step in the direction she wanted to go. Not the most pleasant step, but a step.

The first bundle rustled as Ella pulled it from the trunk, fabric wrapped in tissue paper. She undid the paper carefully. It was white brocade silk, for her wedding dress. Ella held it up for Mother to see.

"Good. Probably the most important thing. We need to take it to the dressmaker. Bring it here."

Mother put down the pen and waved Ella over. She took the cloth and pulled it to arm's length three times, then folded it.

"I think it should be enough. We will see what the dressmaker says. We'll want her to make it loose."

Mother caught Ella's eye.

Ella repeated Ede's words silently to herself, and touched the necklace, which hung hidden under her blouse. She would not rise to this taunt, this reference to the corset scene.

"Yes, Mother."

Mother nodded. "If we were not in such a hurry to get you married, we could have Dulcy make your gown."

Another taunt. Dulcy was THE dressmaker in Vienna. Mother was saying if you were a good daughter, you could have a nice gown. Now you will have only a good-enough gown, made by the local seamstress, who did mending most of the time.

116

Ella touched the necklace.

"Yes, Mother."

"If it is not enough, we will save it for Clara and get you other material." Mother wrote on her paper. "We'll have to see what we can get here."

"When is Clara coming home?" Ella missed Clara, who was still at Grandmother's.

"I'm not sure. I've sent word to Grandmother to send her home when it's convenient, when she has to send something here anyway."

It wasn't that far to Grandmother's, just two hours by cart. Mother didn't seem to want Clara here.

"Will she need a new dress for the wedding?"

"Yes, yes." Mother nodded approvingly. "Yes. That is a good point. I have an old dress. The dressmaker can use that material to make a dress for Clara. But she will need a little time to do that." She wrote on her paper again. "Rewrap this and put it on the bed."

Ella did as she was told and took the next parcel out of the trunk.

An hour later, Ella pulled the first piece of silver from the trunk.

"We will need to get the engraving done." Mother wrote on the paper. "But that does not need to be done before the wedding."

Ella placed the last piece of silver on the table. Mother counted and recounted. Ella wondered whether she liked counting, she seemed to spend so much time doing it.

When the counting was done and everything was replaced in the trunk, Mother locked it.

Mother leaned back in her chair, reading through her list, making notes here and there.

"I think we need another tablecloth, napkins, and we certainly need another layette."

Ella sighed. Mother expected her to knit another baby jacket, pants, cap, socks, mittens, and hat.

"Mother, babies don't come so soon."

Mother's laugh had a morose tone. "You'd be surprised how quickly they come."

"Really?" She looked at her mother.

Mother sat taller, rolling her shoulders. "Yes, yes. Go fetch my knitting basket. I will help. It won't take so long, with two of us working."

Ella stared at her mother. She considered knitting an onerous task, one that Mother demanded she do. She almost considered it a punishment. And here her mother was offering to help.

"Thank you!"

"Yes, yes." Mother smiled at Ella. "I should spend some time with my daughter, my reformed daughter, who is about to become a wife."

Budapest Plans

The next day Ede and Ella walked side by side to the top of a hill on the outskirts of Nagykanizsa. They said little. When they had reached the crest Ede spread a blanket in the shade of an old oak tree. They settled on the cover, Ede, pulling her close, kissing her, stroking her cheek.

Sometime later Ella rolled on her back and looked up. "What a beautiful old tree."

"A little gnarled, I'd say."

"Yes, when you get old, you get gnarled." She pulled a strand of her hair loose and rolled it between her fingers. "And interesting."

He laughed. "You are already quite interesting. I hope I can stand how interesting you will become when you are old and gnarled."

She tried to frown, but she knew he could see her grin.

"How are the wedding plans coming?"

"Mother is being as difficult as she can, now that I am not completely under her control. But I count the days, only 62 more days."

She picked up a twig and peeled the bark back. She didn't need to think of Mother; she could think about the future.

"Only 62 days and then Budapest." She looked up from her twig. "Where will we live?"

"We'll stay in a hotel until we can find an apartment." His hand rested on her knee. "We have to find a home that we both like, with room for lots of books, and a place for both of us to work."

"Do you know where that might be?"

"Not yet. Finding our home will be our first adventure."

"And the next one?"

"We'll have to see. My professor in Leipzig gave me a letter of introduction to a fellow, Oszkár Jászi. He's an editor of a journal, *The Twentieth Century*."

"What's it about."

"In general, it's about the best way to change Hungary, to turn it from an Oriental country to a modern Western country." He looked at her, his lips turned down in a pretend frown. "I'll give you an issue, one that I have from my professor, if you promise your mother won't burn it."

She loved him for teasing her, but she wasn't going to let him know. "Funny."

He extracted a bundle from his pocket and smoothed it out. The cover was cream colored. Across the top, in bold letters, the words spelt out *The Twentieth Century*. The articles in this issue were listed below the title.

Ella read the first item, "SOCIALISM." She looked at Ede. "What's Socialism?"

"It is a way to organize society so that all people share in the wealth of the community."

"Is that possible?"

"Maybe."

"How would you do it?"

"I'm not sure, Kis Maria, of many questions." He was smiling at her, but she knew that he was uncomfortable, that he didn't have all the answers.

She sighed. She had not thought about society, about how it was organized. Her world had been languages and reading, Mother and how to defy her. But maybe this world, this new world, this world of change was what she needed.

Ede patted her knee.

"I'm not sure how to change our country. But, for me, the most important thing is the way we treat women."

"Really?"

"Yes. That's more than half the population, treated like servants... or maybe brood mares."

Ella thought of the chestnut mare.

"And if we could harness women's power, their brain power, their imagination, their talent...."

"Yes, yes."

"Well, that is what I want to do. And I know that is what you want to do. You've wanted it ever since you were four...."

"Maybe even before then."

He laughed. "I don't think changing women's role is so very complicated."

"Really?"

"Yes. Just educate women, allow them to have good careers, allow them to vote."

"Not complicated, but would people agree?"

"Probably not at first. But once you explain how it will make everyone's life better, that not just women will be better off, but men will be too, and children, and society as a whole. When people understand this, then they will agree. "

Ella wondered whether people would listen. Would Father listen? Probably not.

Father approved of Ede because he would be a lawyer. But would Ede have time for his project if he also was a lawyer?

"Can you do all this and be a lawyer too?"

"A lawyer?"

"Father said you were going to be a lawyer."

"Let him think that. We want a nice happy wedding, a quiet

trip to Budapest, so we can start our real work."

She didn't think she could be happier.

Knitting

Mother and Ella settled in Ella's room. Mother started on the baby jacket, while Ella worked on the baby blanket.

"Yes, my daughter. You have changed since your betrothal. We should have done this long ago."

"I am happy."

It was true, but perhaps not for the reason Mother thought.

Now that Mother seemed mellow, Ella dared to ask a question. "Do we really need to make all these baby things? Babies don't need to come right away."

"It only takes nine months," Mother looked up at her smiling. "And you might not feel so well during those months."

She looked down at her work.

"Those terrible months."

"But, I thought there were ways to..." Ella wasn't sure of the right words, the words Ede had used, "to postpone the babies."

"Na." Mother shook her head. "No. I know there are people who say that. But they don't work."

She looked up at her daughter again, a scolding frown on her face. "Besides, those methods are a sin."

"Oh." Ella was not going to contradict her mother. Only 61 more days until the wedding.

"Ya." Mother consulted the pattern, written on a tired yellow scrap of paper. "A sin."

Mother's lips compressed as she looked at Ella. "Think of what happened to Therese."

"Oh, you mean that." Ella felt the weight of the necklace

under her blouse and took courage from it. "But I thought that there were other ways."

Mother snorted. "Well, if the husband leaves you alone. Yes. But men will not do that."

She gave her daughter a knowing smile and shook her head. "Not healthy young men like Ede."

"Oh."

Mother looked beyond Ella, her smile fading.

"Men, when the mood arises, are beasts."

That seemed extreme to Ella. "Beasts?"

"Oh, my dear daughter, a woman's life is not...."

She dropped her knitting on her lap and took a handkerchief from her sleeve and wiped her eyes.

"Men are beasts."

Ella stared. She could not believe this. "Not Ede."

"Oh, my poor, poor dear. That is what I thought just before my wedding. Not my husband. Everyone thought he was such a kind, generous, gentle man."

Mother dabbed her eyes again.

"But he turned into something else."

Ella had never seen this side of her mother. She had never seen her cry, but now the soft sobs spilled out, one after another.

Mother inhaled, blew her nose and tucked her kerchief in her sleeve.

"Just listen to me, let him do whatever he wants, no matter how disgusting or sinful. He is bigger than you and stronger. If you resist he might...." She quivered as she let her breath out. "... he will hurt you."

Ella could not take her eyes off Mother. "Father?"

"Yes, your father." Her mother held her stare. "A beast!"

"A beast?" What had happened?

Mother took out her handkerchief again and dabbed her eyes.

"But let us talk of something more cheerful."

After stuffing the cloth up her sleeve, she picked up her knitting and began stitching the little jacket.

"Your dress will look stunning. You are quite beautiful my daughter."

She scanned Ella and smiled.

"I am proud of my beautiful daughter." She sighed. "But I am sorry you will live in Budapest, so far away. Just when we were becoming friends."

Ella swallowed.

She wanted to know what Father had done. She didn't believe her father could hurt anyone.

But why would her mother tell her this if it were not true? Ella had never known her to lie.

And Mother had cried. She had never seen Mother cry before.

"Yes, just when we are becoming friends you move away." Mother stopped stitching and spread the partially completed jacket on her knee, inspecting her work.

"Children are difficult."

Ella knew that meant her. "I'm sorry Mother."

Mother looked up and smiled. "Yes, yes, you were difficult, but you are changed now."

Again she stitched.

"But I mean something else. It's difficult. Your husband lies with you, then you are sick with child. Will your husband leave you alone, just because you are carrying his child and cannot keep food down? No. He demands his desires be met. Half of the time you lose the child. Maybe because of his demands?" Her eyes welled up.

It was as if a dam had been topped. Ella had never heard these things before, had never seen her mother as vulnerable.

Mother's words kept streaming forth, as if she were unable to stop them.

"But if the child comes, and it comes with pain, horrible wrenching pain, oceans of pain that sweep over you again and again and again. Because sex is a sin and God punishes, though I'm not sure why He punishes the woman and not the man."

She dropped her work as her hand flew to her mouth. She crossed herself, her eyes closed.

"God forgive me."

Again the sobs, the mopping of the eyes. Ella rested her hands on her lap, her eyes fixed on Mother.

Again Mother brought herself under control with sighs, quivering as she exhaled.

"Let me tell you one thing. When you have a baby, get a wet nurse."

"A wet nurse?"

"Yes, yes." She pursed her lips. "A wet nurse and a nanny. That way you don't fall in love with your child."

"I see." But Ella didn't see. Why would a mother not want to love her child?

Like a little ray of sunshine peeking from the clouds, a gentle smile played on Mother's lips. "Did I ever tell you about my first, my little Erzsébet?"

Ella shook her head.

"I try not to think of her. She was a darling. Pudgy and sweet, with auburn curls."

Mother rubbed her hands along her skirt, looking at Ella.

"About the same color as yours, maybe just a touch lighter. Hair so curly that it shone like a halo when the sun struck it. She had a dimple when she laughed and was so shy. She hid in

126

my skirts whenever anyone else approached her."

"She sounds lovely."

"She was." Mother's face brightened. "I loved her so. She was about two, strong and healthy. We did so much together, I almost didn't need a nanny. And I nursed her. From the day she was born. I loved looking at her when she sucked, her little eyes shut tight when she was tiny, and then as she got older, her gaze would wander. Sometimes she would look into my eyes, as if she were saying thank you."

"So you liked nursing her?"

"Yes."

"Then why are you telling me to use a wet nurse when I have a baby?"

"Because."

Mother withdrew her handkerchief again, which must have been sodden by now.

"Because."

Her body shook.

"Because Father wanted another child, he wanted a boy. He said he needed a boy to help him with his business. He was angry with me, saying I was doing something so that I would not conceive again." Mother gulped and coughed. "Of course, I would not do that. It is sinful."

She looked past Ella, tears on her cheeks, her chin, on her bodice. She no longer tried to mop them up.

"But why were you not getting pregnant?"

"Yes, yes. Father consulted the doctor and asked just that. The doctor said I might not be conceiving because I was still nursing Erzsébet."

"Really? Is that true?"

"Oh, I don't know."

Mother sobbed so, Ella took out her handkerchief and went

to her, wiping her face.

Mother tried to smile, but that seemed only to cause more wails. "All I know is that Father commanded me to stop nursing her."

Ella put her handkerchief in Mother's hand and fetched a glass of water from the wash stand.

Mother tried to drink a bit, but she coughed, the liquid running down her chin. She pushed the glass back into Ella's hand.

"I tried to sneak in little sips when Father was at work, so he paid the nanny to watch me. Can you imagine? The nanny was spying on me! I tried to let her go, but Father would not allow it."

The sobs erupted again, one after another.

"So I stopped." Dabbing and sobs. "Erzsébet didn't understand. She cried. She wouldn't eat. She grew thin and pale."

Mother put her head in her hands, sobbing, her knitting falling to the floor.

Ella strained to hear Mother's next words.

"She died within the month. I cried and would not speak to my husband. I would not allow him near me. He had killed my Erzsébet. In the end he... well he had his way with me. And I was pregnant."

Mother's sobs where constant now and seemed beyond control.

Ella sat beside her mother, holding her and rocking her.

Nightmares

Mother had finally calmed down and Ella asked Cook for tea. Mother smiled at Ella, a weak smile, almost as if she were ashamed.

She tried to take up the knitting again, but her hand shook so that Ella suggested they stop for today.

"I will finish this before the wedding," she said, not knowing how she could possibly do that, but it seemed to calm Mother.

Mother's confession made Ella uncomfortable. She wanted her angry grim mother back, someone she could hate, but now she had to console her.

"I am sorry, Mother, for the trouble I have caused."

Mother nodded. Weakly.

Ella said, "I love you."

Maybe this was not true, but telling her so would not hurt anything and might help somehow.

Mother's face was pale. The earlier blush from her crying had drained away. "I love you too, Daughter."

They passed the afternoon quietly, Ella reading to Mother from the bible.

> Come unto me, all ye that labour and are heavy laden, and I will give you rest.
> Take my yoke upon you, and learn of me; for I am meek and lowly in heart: and ye shall find rest unto your souls.
> For my yoke is easy, and my burden is light.

Ella had never read to Mother before, but it seemed to give her comfort and it allowed Ella to escape into her own thoughts.

That night, as Ella lay in bed, she tried to forget her mother's words, but they raced through her mind again and again.

"Do whatever he says, no matter how disgusting or sinful."

She rolled over adjusting her pillows.

"He is stronger and bigger than you."

She touched the necklace, still around her neck.

He was stronger than she was, but he was her friend. He had always been her friend. He would not hurt her.

"A healthy young man like Ede has his appetites."

She turned on her other side.

Yes, Ede had admitted his appetites. And he had said that was the reason he wanted to marry her.

"No matter how disgusting and sinful."

Ella didn't care about sinful. She wasn't sure what was sinful.

She thought of the stallion's penis, long and straight. She thought of the mare: calm, quiet, her head a little down, her neck stretched out. She did not seem to mind. Or was the mare just following Mother's advice: do whatever he says because he is bigger and stronger than you and can hurt you?

No.

She rubbed her thumb across the emerald, feeling the edges of the stone's facets.

No.

Ede was different. He would never hurt her.

But what of Father? Did she think Father would hurt her?

Or her mother?

Ede's words echoed: "Maybe our children will have such beautiful eyes."

A tear dribbled down her chin.

She knew now she could not marry, could not have children.

She had to escape.

She shivered as she rose from bed and put on her blouse and skirt. She threw some underthings into her satchel, put in her *Huckleberry Finn* and *Tale of Two Cities*.

She saw the shawl Ede had given her. She hesitated. Should she take that too, given to her by a man?

Somehow she wanted it, knew that it would comfort her, even if it was from the man she was running from. She put it on top of the other things.

She would leave. She would run away, like she had planned.

But she must not go to Budapest. Ede would go to Budapest.

She would have to go to Vienna.

She needed money, for the train ticket and some more, for... she wasn't sure what would happen once she got to Vienna. She would have to find a job.

As a nanny?

Or a tutor?

She could find something.

But she needed money. She took the pile of coins she had "saved" from her marketing trips. That would not be enough.

Where could she get more money?

Her fingers felt the key fob Miklos had given her.

The keys!

Mother had a drawer full of money for the household expenses. It might even have more than usual because of the upcoming wedding. She would take the money in the drawer.

Stealing was wrong.

Should she really do this?

Mother's words echoed in her head. "He had his way with me."

She must leave. She couldn't marry. Stealing was wrong, but forcing marriage was a worse wrong.

She took the fob, looking for a small key that might fit the money drawer.

The Loan

The oil lamp cast a gloomy light in the pantry as Ella set to work trying keys. She hardly dared to breathe, worried that she might wake Cook or Maid, who slept in the little room next to the pantry.

Her hands grew sweaty as she tried one key after another. None of them fit that well, so she wasn't sure she had rejected the key that would open the drawer. She looked at the fob. There were only two small keys left. She tried the next key. It slid in almost all the way, but then stopped. She rocked it this way and that, but it would go no farther.

What would she do if she couldn't get into the drawer? Might she force it open?

No!

That would make too much noise. It would wake Cook or Maid for sure.

She took the last key and slid it into the hole. It went in. All the way. She inhaled and held her breath. She turned it slowly hearing the latch release. She exhaled, feeling her shoulders relax.

She slid the drawer open. It had bills and change. She riffled through the stack of bills. Should she take it all? No. Mother would realize right away that something was wrong. Let her count it. Let her take her time and count it. That would give Ella more time to escape.

Taking a stack of bills, the larger denominations, she closed the drawer without bothering to lock it. She tiptoed back to her room.

Mother's sobs from yesterday still echoed in her mind. She was done with all that. Goodbye to the fights and the craziness. She would go to Vienna and start a new life, a reasonable, rational, good life.

A whimper escaped her lips.

She was wrong to steal this money. And Mother might blame Cook or Maid for taking it. Then they would be let go.

Like Therese.

Well, not like Therese, but without a recommendation. She didn't mind stealing itself, but hurting Cook or Maid? She didn't really know Maid. She was fond of Cook, who had always been with the family.

If she was to start a new rational life, she had better start it now. And causing Cook or Maid trouble, real trouble, poverty, shame.... No. She could not do it.

But she must leave. And she needed the money.

She grabbed a pen and a sheet of paper and scribbled:

> *Mother,*
> *I cannot marry. I have gone. I have taken money from the drawer. I will pay back this money, as soon as I can.*
> *Love,*
> *Ella*

She stopped writing. Her mother's cries tore through her. Poor Mother!

She laid the paper in the middle of the table.

Leaving the note had cost her time.

She must leave now, before someone got up.

She pushed the money into her satchel, just underneath her shawl, next to her under things and her books. She slipped several large bills in her pocket, for easier access. She didn't want to fumble for money at the train station.

Ella walked to the front door, bumping into the coat stand in the entry hall. It rattled and looked like it might tumble. She steadied it.

The door was locked.

Her hands shook as she tried the first large key, which didn't even fit the keyhole. She tried the next and it went in all the way. She turned it and heard the happy sound of the tumblers dropping.

She pushed the door as gently as she could until it opened just enough for her to go through. Dropping the fob in her satchel, she pulled the door shut. She didn't relock it. They would see her note soon enough, no point in locking the door in the pretense that nothing was amiss.

She took the stairs by twos, trying to be quiet.

Now that she was out of the house, she needed to hurry.

She walked down Fő út, past Ede's house. A lump grew in her throat.

Dear Ede.

Or Ede the beast?

She touched the necklace, which still hung under her blouse. She should have left that. That was a gift to Ede's wife and she no longer considered herself his wife. That was like stealing too. But she could not turn back now. If she did she would be married. No. She would find a way to return it to him.

She steadied herself as she turned down Sörház út, much narrower than Fő út, walking past the City Hall and the Iron Man House.

The morning air was fresh and cool. Birds chirped and twittered, telling the sun it was time to rise. This was the first day of her new life. It would be a good life, a worthy life, a life in which she did something of value.

Not like Mother's life.

She entered the train station, her steps echoing as she walked across the empty high-ceilinged hall. She knew there were early trains for Vienna, though she was not sure when they left. She hoped that she could get one soon.

"Good morning Miss Weisel."

She looked into the stationmaster's mustachioed face.

"What is the bride doing here so early?" he grinned at her.

"Oh, Mr. Kovacs, I must go to Budapest. My Aunt needs help."

Oh no. She had misspoken. She had said Budapest. Of course that had been her first plan and she hadn't thought through another one. But it was done. Now she had to carry it through. Maybe when she got to Budapest she could take another train to Vienna. That would be better anyhow, in case Mother sent Miklos after her.

"You'd think Mrs. Weisel could send someone other than the bride," the stationmaster said as he stroked his long mustache, turning the right tip up just a bit.

"I'm Auntie's favorite, and she isn't feeling well."

"You are a devoted girl, doing that for your aunt."

Was that a gleam of sarcasm she saw in his eyes? The whole town probably knew of all the turmoil that preceded this hasty wedding.

"She's my favorite too."

"OK, well it's a round-trip ticket to Budapest then."

"Oh, no."

She didn't want to spend more than she had to, but he would expect a round trip ticket, since she would need to return for her wedding.

"I'm not sure how we are coming back."

"OK." His chuckle sounded like a taunt to Ella's ear. "But the train is the fastest way."

His grin grew wider. "You don't want to miss your own wedding."

She nodded and tried to smile, hating him all the more for his little joke.

"One first-class ticket to Budapest," he said.

She wished that she could get a second or even a third class ticket, to save money. But of course Mr. Weisel's daughter would only travel first class.

He quoted the price.

Ella reached into her pocket and pulled out three bills. She wished she had taken more money. She wished she had counted what she had taken before she left. She begged her hand not to shake.

The stationmaster handed her a ticket.

"Off you go. Track 2. The Budapest train leaves immediately and you don't want to miss it. There won't be another one until noon."

Again the broad grin and the twinkle in his eye.

The Ride to Budapest

Ella ran onto the platform. The train was huffing steam and the conductor, calling all aboard, looked up and down the platform for late comers. He gave her a hand as she climbed the stairs. Again he looked in both directions and then looked at her.

"Who is traveling with you, Miss?"

"I'm alone."

His eyes narrowed. "I see." He took her satchel. "Wench."

She inhaled sharply. She wasn't sure what that meant, but she didn't like his familiar tone, and she didn't know how to respond. She ignored him, walking quickly down the narrow corridor.

He followed. "This compartment," he said.

The compartment seated six, but there was no one else in it. The conductor started to put her satchel in an overhead cabinet.

"I'll keep that with me." She didn't want her things out of her sight.

He nodded, handed the bag to her, and closed the door as he departed.

She settled on the cushioned seat, covered in rich brocade. There were seats across from her. Above the seats, the walls bulged in curves. These hid bunks that could be opened up at night, but this train would be in Budapest by early afternoon.

The whistle blew and the train lurched forward.

The compartment provided her the privacy she had craved, the privacy to count her money. She drew out the bills and change, counting.

Counting like her mother.

The train ticket alone had been more than she had expected. She could not purchase a ticket to Vienna when she got to Budapest.

At least not a first class ticket.

But maybe a second class ticket?

She didn't know. She didn't even know how to find out. Were the prices posted? She had never paid for anything, except at the market.

Maybe it would be better to stay in Budapest, just for a day or two, to figure out what she would do next. If she did she would have to stay somewhere away from her aunt, who lived in the Buda hills. She would stay across the Danube in Pest.

She had always wanted to explore Pest. She had been there once, with her aunt, who had taken her to the city park, with its zoo and lake, and the display of castles. It had been fun when she was nine, but she was convinced there were more interesting places to go in Pest.

She got out her Huck and tried to read about his escape from Aunt Sally's. She hadn't used her bed linens, as he did. But one didn't do that kind of thing in Nagykanizsa. What if someone saw her climbing down from the third story, right onto Fő út, her satchel hanging from her arm, her skirts flying?

The thought made her laugh. She would get through this. She would conquer Budapest. That is, Vienna.

She looked out the window and caught a glimpse of Lake Balaton as the train sped by. Lake Balaton, with sail boats and beaches.

She remembered an excursion with Father and Miklos the summer when she was ten. Ede had come too. They swam in the lake and walked along the shore. They read to each other at night. They went out after dark and named the constellations.

Oh, Ede!

She felt the weight of the necklace against her skin, but her mother's words echoed in her head: "He had his way with me."

She straightened her spine. She would need to find work, a way to support herself.

How does one find work?

She had never thought about that question. She had seen Mother interview maids, cooks, nannies, even companions, but she had no idea how Mother found those people to interview. Or how the applicants got the interview.

Did one just go to the place one wanted to work and ask?

Supposing this was how it was done, where would she go?

She knew she wanted to translate. She knew she was good enough to translate French or German or English. Probably there were plenty of people who could translate German; many people in Hungary spoke German as their mother tongue. But French? Or even better English. The only person she knew, other than herself, who could speak English was Ede.

And Alexa, of course. But she was in Chicago now.

Oh, Ede! She bit her lip.

She would not think about Ede.

How does one find a job translating from English? Or to English? Who would need that? Maybe a place that had English speaking people. An embassy? A business? Or maybe a newspaper?

The train rocked gently and the sound mesmerized her. Her lids closed as she thought of newspapers. Where were newspapers printed? Or written. She recalled the journal that Ede had shown her, *The Twentieth Century*, its cream cover, with the list of articles and writers. There was Ede's name. The title of an article: *Ede has His Way with Ella*. She turned to the page. Words, blurry words, ran down the page.

She smelled something sour.

Whiskey.

She felt a hand on her throat, a hand working its way under her collar.

She opened her eyes.

Eyes stared into hers, blue watery eyes. Lips pressed against hers as the hand undid a button at the top of her blouse.

She screamed and pushed the eyes, the lips, the hands away.

She pushed as hard as she could, flaying her arms and legs.

The man, the fat old man backed away, his hands held out in front of him.

She grabbed her satchel, pulled the door to the compartment open, and ran down the corridor. The swaying train knocked her off balance so that she bounced between the outer wall of the car and the compartments.

She reached the end of the car, which had a door connecting to the next car. She twisted the handle and pulled the door open.

The heat of the day blew in her face. What had been the quiet click clack of the train was now a roar.

As she looked back over her shoulder she saw the back of the fat man at the door of her compartment, his arms gesticulating. The conductor, facing the man, looked at her.

She stepped onto the platform, opened the door on the other side, and closed it behind her. When she entered the next car, the roar hushed. It was a third class car, the seats in neat rows. People looked up at her. She put her hand to her throat to cover the unbuttoned collar. Several rows down three nuns sat. Ella hurried to them.

"Sisters, may I sit with you?"

The Sisters

The nun on the right, the one with the steely eyes, the graying brows, and the long straight nose, nodded, then pushed her chin forward indicating Ella should sit next to the nun on the other bench. The sister on the opposite bench, a young woman, maybe only a year or two older than Ella, moved over, making more room.

Ella sat down on the bench, a hard wooden surface, not cushioned like the seats in the first class cabin. Better a hard safe seat than a cushy chair and the man with watery blue eyes and sour breath.

"You are in trouble, child?" The nun with steely eyes asked. Her face was stony.

"Non, non," Ella decided to speak in French, hoping the sisters did not speak it. That way she would have to answer fewer questions.

"You are French?" The stern sister unfortunately did speak French.

Ella wasn't sure how well. Suddenly she was unsure of her own accent.

"Oui." She cast her eyes down, trying to avoid the sister's penetrating eyes.

"Your name?" the older nun asked.

She couldn't give her real name. She didn't want anyone to know who she was. She didn't want to be sent back to Nagykanizsa.

"Therese." It was the first name that came to mind.

"I see." The nun's voice had that imperious tone, like Mother Mary Theresa's at the convent school, like an abbess. Ella knew that mother superior tone. It was used again and again, drilling, wheedling, digging for the truth. It did not lead to a good place.

"Do you have a family name Therese?"

Ella could not recall Therese's family name. Maybe that was just as well. She wouldn't want to name Therese. It might give this Mother Superior clues to who she really was.

But she needed a family name. A French family name. She remembered the name of the doctor in *A Tale of Two Cities*. "Manette. Therese Manette."

"And who is traveling with you, Miss Manette?"

Just like the stationmaster and the conductor, Mother Superior wanted to know why a young girl would be traveling alone.

At that moment, Ella wished Therese was with her. If Therese were here, she would not have been attacked by that man with the sour breath. Yes, perhaps her mother had reason to hire a companion. Perhaps young women were only safe when traveling with a companion. She had not valued Therese when she had her and now, when she really needed her....

"I am traveling alone, to see my aunt in Budapest. She is ill."

"A French girl has an aunt in Budapest?"

"Yes, yes. She married a Hungarian."

"I see."

Mother Superior folded her hands in her lap. Mother Mary Theresa had done that too, as if it helped lay traps for lying students.

Where are you from, Therese Manette?"

"Paris." The answer was automatic. Therese had been from Paris.

"A beautiful city."

"Yes."

"Where did you live?"

Ella wished she had paid more attention when Therese had talked about her home. She wished she had paid more attention to the map of Paris Therese had shown her. She needed an answer. "Champs-Élysées."

Ella glanced at Mother Superior quickly, who nodded. "I see." Her lips stretched in a frown. "A French girl, traveling alone, whose Hungarian is better than her French."

The nun's words were sharp. "A French girl who lives on the Champs-Élysées."

Ella looked down and bit her lip. Saying anything else would only make things worse.

"I would say that you are not where you are supposed to be and you are not doing what you are supposed to be doing."

Ella held her breath, looking down.

"Button your blouse, French girl." The words were hushed but biting.

Ella's fingers went to her throat, fumbling to push the button through the button hole. Mother Superior would see her shaking hands and know she was right.

"Who are you?" Mother Superior demanded.

Somehow the command gave Ella courage, the courage she had when she defied Mother. She met Mother Superior's eyes. She did not blink. She did not say a word.

"Whoever you are, you shall come to the convent when we get to Budapest. Once you are there we will discover the truth."

Ella thought of the time she spent on her knees in the convent school, Mother Mary Theresa demanding she confess her sins. She thought of the burning rap of the ruler across her knuckles when she made a mistake in her tatting. She

144

remembered how sister held up her embroidery, showing everyone the uneven puckered work. Ella knew she must not go to the convent. But she also needed a safe place to sit until the train arrived in Budapest.

She touched Ede's emerald under her blouse and planned her escape.

Arrival

The train slowed as it entered the outskirts of Budapest, a landscape she remembered from her visits to her aunt. People began to gather their belongings.

Ella caught the Mother Superior's eye. "Might I get your things for you?"

The nun nodded and pointed out three identical black cases in the overhead bin.

Ella had already guessed which ones they were. She carefully pulled one down setting it between her and the benches where the sisters sat. Then the next and the last one, setting them down next to the first, so they formed a row between herself and the sisters.

She nodded towards the lavatory and set off at a calm pace. When she got to the lavatory, she looked over her shoulder. The older nun was handing one of the cases to the youngest sister.

Ella pulled the door between cars open and rushed across the platform, her satchel over her shoulder. She let the car door slam behind her in the next car and ran down the aisle as the train slowed.

She crossed over to the next car, where she pulled her shawl from her bag, wrapping it over her head and around her neck letting the ends drape down her back as the peasant women did.

By this time, the train had stopped. People crowded the aisle, but she bustled to the back of the car. She looked back, hoping not to see the nuns' black head covering. Everyone was now pushing toward the doors and Ella joined them, not wanting to be the last one on the train, not wanting to be easily spotted. She concentrated on staying in the middle of the crowd, resisting the temptation to look for the nuns.

The mass of people flowed off the car and walked along the train toward the terminal. The nuns' car was closer to the terminal, so if they tried to locate her, they would stand out walking against the crowd.

That was true as long as they were still walking to the terminal. Once they had reached it, the nuns might wait and try to find her. She added a limp to her walk and sloughed to one side, hoping that this, along with her shawl might serve as a disguise.

A young couple just ahead of her chatted in Croat. Ella caught snatches of their conversation, though her Croat was meager. They were going to an inn, close to the train station. They talked about whether they might walk rather than find a carriage or take a tram. They stopped to look at a map.

Ella stopped next to them. "New to Budapest?"

She used as few words as possible, not wanting to stretch her Croat knowledge too far.

"No Hungarian?"

The young man shook his head.

"No German?" He wore a suit, new, but ill-fitting. The woman was in a dark dress, with her pretty black hair peeking from under a head scarf.

He held his fingers up, indicating he had just a little.

Ella switched to German "Where are you going?"

The man pointed to a spot on the map.

"Yes, yes." Ella nodded. "I see."

"Walk?" The man asked, apparently asking whether their

destination was near.

Ella looked at their luggage. He carried a little case, she a carpet bag. The inn was not that far away and it was early afternoon.

She nodded. "I will show you. I will walk with you."

The man sighed and put his arm around the young woman. "Thank you."

They started toward the terminal again.

Ella scanned the crowd looking for the three nuns. There they were, walking ahead of them, some distance away, but walking slowly, looking this way and that.

Ella swallowed. She didn't want to catch up with them, so she tried to walk a little slower, but the Croat couple kept up their pace and she wanted to stay with them.

They were slowly gaining on the nuns.

Now ten meters behind them, now five.

Ella talked to the Croat couple, making herself not look in the direction of the nuns.

"Where do you come from?"

The man smiled. "Kiskanizsa."

Kiskanizsa was really part of Nagykanizsa, the two towns having merged in the last decades, but this couple clearly thought of it as separate.

"I have a new job in a brewery. I had a job at the Kanizsa Brewery and they needed people in Budapest, so I have come," the man said.

Ella nodded. She wanted them to keep talking, so that the nuns would think they belonged together.

"Where will you live?"

"We will have to find a place. They say it is hard to find rooms in Budapest."

Ella felt a hand on her shoulder.

"Where are you going, French girl?"

Names

Ella swung around to face the Mother Superior. "How dare you!" Ella said in German, pushing the hand from her shoulder. She could see a flash of uncertainty in the nun's eyes.

"Who are you?" Ella demanded.

The Croat man stepped between Ella and the nun. Mother Superior squinted and backed away.

"Who?" The Croat man asked.

"I don't know." Ella shook her head and the three resumed their walk toward the exit.

Ella resisted the urge to see if the nuns had retreated. Instead she talked to the couple stretching her knowledge of Croat to its limit. The woman smiled when Ella searched for the word for beer.

Having been in Buda many times to visit her aunt, Ella knew where the inn was situated with respect to the train station, but she had never walked in this neighborhood. Her family always hired a coach and was driven into the Buda Hills, where her aunt lived. She hoped the route she chose would be safe. At least she was not walking alone.

Trees lined the street outside the train station, but they were young and spindly and did not provide much shade. Ella wished she could remove the shawl, but didn't dare to, fearing the sisters might yet find her.

She walked with the Croat couple, guiding them the several blocks to their destination. They thanked her profusely. She nodded and smiled.

Once they had entered the inn, Ella looked around. She wanted to go to Pest, that part of the city on the East side of the Danube.

She didn't want to accidentally meet her aunt, though that was unlikely even if she stayed in Buda. Aunt Ilona rarely went out.

Still, something drew her to Pest. It was the new side, the modern side, the place where the better Hungary that Ede talked about would be born. She had memorized the way when looking at the Croats' map.

She headed down Krisztina körút toward the Danube. The short thin trees provided no protection from the summer sun and she was hot with her shawl draped about her.

Looking around she noted fewer women with covered heads, so she let the material fall to her shoulders. A slight breeze dried the moisture on her cheeks, cooling them. They felt gritty with dried sweat.

Her stomach rumbled. She promised herself she would stop at a café, but only once she reached Pest.

She thought about Therese as she walked. What was her last name? Somehow, now that she was dead, that she had died so terribly, it seemed wrong that Ella could not remember her last name.

Biss... Bisset. She was Therese Bisset.

That was better.

What about Cook? She had a real name. Yes, of course, it was Maria.

Why did she call Maria Cook? She thought back to when she was three. She had called her Cook because she was the cook.

But there was another reason, if she could just remember.

Yes, Maria was such a common name, and Mother had hired a maid called Maria. So Ella called Maria, the cook, Cook and

Maria, the maid, Maid, so as not to confuse the two.

Maria the maid hadn't stayed long. Maids never did in Mother's house, always being accused of being too slow, not thorough enough, or, worst of all, stealing.

She wondered where all the maids went once Mother let them go without a reference. They couldn't take "a loan" from the money drawer, like she had. They didn't have the keys. And they didn't have her "market money" because they were not usually sent to market.

What did they do?

Did they manage to find another position? Or did they go home to their family?

She remembered the letter to Therese, telling her not to bring more mouths to feed.

Therese and the maids, Ella realized, had a tenuous hold on security.

The intersection ahead was at an obtuse angle. That must be Alagút utca, where she had to turn to get to the Chain Bridge.

She walked around the corner and stopped.

A tall stone archway, maybe 20 meters tall, stood half a block away. Had she taken a wrong turn?

She walked more slowly as she approached the opening and looked through what was a tunnel. At the far end she could see the Chain Bridge, the one she had seen so often on postcards Aunt Ilona had sent.

She was on the right path.

But the tunnel looked forbidding.

Might another fat man with sour breath lurk there?

It was not that long, maybe three blocks.

She swallowed her fears, entered, and walked along the pedestrian path to the side of the tunnel.

It was hot and humid and it stank. Horses and other draft

animals clearly did not curb their needs while in it.

She quickened her pace and placed the end of her shawl over her nose and mouth, hoping to keep the wretched stench from her nostrils. Her steps echoed on the tiled walls.

When she reached the end of the tunnel, she inhaled, savoring the little wind that cooled her and wafted away the acrid odors. The bridge towered before her, the famous bridge, guarded by two huge lions on either side. All Hungarian children were told that those lions had no tongues, but she was not going to investigate today. She wanted to get to Pest, to get to a café.

She kept up her rapid pace, striding toward that goal.

In the middle of the bridge she stopped for just a moment to admire the view of the Parliament building, standing grandly on the banks of the Danube. It was even larger than she had remembered. But then Budapest was the capitol of Hungary. Or at least it was the twin capitol, along with Vienna, of the Austro-Hungarian Empire.

Perhaps such an important city should have a large Parliament building.

It looked prickly, like a dragon with many spikes.

She thought it was more threatening than beautiful.

She started walking again, her steps more confident. Just a few more minutes and she would be on the Pest side.

Then all she had to do was find a café.

The Café

Ella felt her stomach gurgle. She had not eaten anything since yesterday.

She wandered the streets of Pest, looking into cafés, in search of an appropriate place to eat. She didn't know where she could stay tonight, so she wanted to conserve her money.

She gazed into one window, waiters moving from table to table, men in top hats and boys in caps, boys about her age or maybe a little younger, gymnasium boys, sitting at the tables, drinking coffee and eating rolls. The men were talking and smoking pipes and cigars.

This place, with the gymnasium boys, could not be too expensive. She entered the half-full hall and looked around.

Most of the women sat in one section along the wall opposite the door. She sat at a little table among the other women, feeling more comfortable there.

A moment later a waiter appeared, an older man, lean with a long face. He looked her up and down, saying nothing.

"Coffee, rolls, butter." She needed more than this, but it was a start.

A long hand set a cup of steaming black coffee on the table. A small pot of cream followed. Ella poured as much cream into the coffee as the cup would hold. She sipped. The tan liquid filled her mouth with smooth rich flavor.

It was the best coffee she had ever tasted.

The long hand set a basket of rolls and a plate of butter on her table. She took one of the rolls and pulled it apart, tearing off a bite sized piece and spreading sunny yellow butter over it. She chewed the moist yeasty bread. The next bite, from the crusty outside of the roll, with the salty butter and the perfect crunch, was heaven.

She scanned the room.

A cluster of men and boys were seated at a large round table not far from her, talking with great emotion. All heads seemed turned to the man at the far side. Someone would make a comment and he would reply, wiping his forehead with a dingy handkerchief. An older man commented and everyone chuckled. Once the wave of humor passed, the man at the far side put on a serious face and said something, stuffing the handkerchief in his pocket. People nodded. Ella could not understand what was being said above the noise of the high-ceilinged room.

Her eyes drifted. She noticed men sitting by themselves, reading newspapers. She saw one man pick up his paper and walk to the corner of the room where a rack stood. Many papers hanging on poles were arranged on the rack. The man replaced the paper he was reading and took another one.

If he could read papers from the rack, so could she.

Having negotiated her way to the corner, she sorted through the papers. She had never seen so many journals. *Budapesti Szemle, Pesti Hirlap, Magyar Salon*, and on and on. Her eye fell on a cream colored cover. *The Twentieth Century*. The journal Ede had shown her.

Her heart beat faster as she picked up the little journal and took it back to her table. She noticed the address on the cover.

Maybe they would need a translator.

But wouldn't that be where Ede would go?

She couldn't worry about that now. She needed money. She doubted she had enough money for a train ticket to Vienna.

She needed to make money so she could go to Vienna.

Maybe this journal would hire her. And if not this journal, maybe another.

Ella flipped through the pages and then returned to the front page.

The first article listed, "About Socialism," was written by Dr. Ervin Szabó.

Had Ede mentioned his name? She wasn't sure.

She turned to the page and read. Social science, the article explained, described how society was organized based on certain laws about something.

She looked up without seeing anything, trying to comprehend what she had read. She skimmed the words again.

"You're not from Budapest, are you?"

Ella looked up. One of the gymnasium boys sat down across from her. His smile was warm. His bright brown eyes searched her face.

"What makes you think so?"

"To start, women of a certain sort sit here."

"Oh?"

"But you don't look like that sort."

Ella had to smile. At least this young boy realized, even if everyone else in the world didn't – the conductor, sour-breath, the old nun – she was just trying to.... What was she trying to do? She was just trying to be her own person.

But this young man, with his sweet smile, seemed sympathetic.

"How do you know I'm not that sort?" She bit her lip. Maybe she shouldn't have said that. Maybe he would think she was "that sort."

"For one thing, you aren't dressed like a...." He let the sentence hang.

Ella sighed with relief. He didn't seem to have been swayed from his opinion about what sort she was.

"And those women don't spend their time reading *The Twentieth Century*."

"Oh." She wondered what sort of woman did read it.

"And, finally," He grinned as he nodded to her satchel, "that sort doesn't come with their luggage."

She laughed.

"So, I thought, you are a stranger here and must be an interesting stranger."

She nodded. His hair, straight, shiny, parted on the side, was perfectly groomed. His peachy cheeks didn't have a hint of a beard.

"And I thought maybe you could use some help?"

She nodded again. She could use some help. And this youth with his high white collar and tie, with his vest and jacket, seemed kind.

And maybe even safe.

"What are you doing here, Lady of Another Sort?"

She smiled now. "I've run away from home."

His brows raised but his sweet smile remained. "Really?"

She nodded.

His brown eyes held her gaze. "Why?"

"I was to be married."

He nodded, as if he understood everything. "To an ugly fat old man."

Ella thought of Ede. This young fellow resembled Ede, with his earnest eyes and his kind smile.

"No. He is young, handsome and quite... fit."

The boy squinted. "So he was mean? Or nasty? Or cruel?"

"No." She touched the necklace under her blouse. "He is my only friend."

The boy's brows furrowed and he shook his head. "So why did you run away?"

She swallowed. She had already said too much. She could not tell this stranger more, no matter how young he was or how kind his eyes.

"I ask too many questions." He glanced around the room. "But Lady of Another Sort, this is not the place for you."

His gaze came back to her.

"People will get the wrong idea." He stared at her, his smile gone.

"You'd best come home with me."

She shook her head. She should not have told him all this.

At least he did not know her name.

She pushed back her chair to leave.

The Walk to Cecile's Home

The boy touched her hand. "No, no. Don't think I mean anything of the wrong sort." His smile had returned. "I mean come to my home to meet my mother. She will be able to help you."

Ella hesitated. Should she trust this boy? Right now it seemed an appealing option. She was tired and hungry. She didn't know where she would sleep tonight or how to find a room or how much it would cost. This boy's offer was very appealing.

As the young man held the door for Ella, he said, "I'm Mihály."

Lying had gotten Ella in trouble. She would only tell him the truth, or nothing at all. She tilted her head and smiled. "Ella."

The heat of the day had descended on the city. They walked along Váci utca, a narrow street that could barely accommodate the carriages traveling it. The walkways were crowded too, people stopping here and there to look into store windows. Some of the shops had awnings, but they provided little shade and almost no relief from the sun's heat.

"And what were you reading, Ella?"

"Something called 'On Socialism'."

"You are interested in socialism?"

"My friend," she bit her lip, not wanting to say too much about Ede. "He talked about it and I wanted to understand what he had said."

"Your friend who you are not going to marry?"

She looked at Mihály. An impish grin had spread across his lips. She shouldn't have said that. She didn't want this inquisitive boy to know more, so she ignored his question.

"The trouble is, reading that article was like reading a different language. It had words I don't know."

"Yes, well, I'm not surprised," the boy said. "Probably they don't speak much about socialism outside of Budapest."

"They speak of it in Budapest?"

"Oh, in Budapest, yes." He smiled. "In Paris and Berlin, in Moscow and London and New York. In most cities. But not in the Hungarian countryside so much, I would guess. And maybe not among your people."

She was miffed by his condescension, but he was right. In Nagykanizsa she had not heard of socialism, except that one time Ede had discussed it.

"Can you explain it to me?"

"I'm not sure I can. I think it might mean different things to different people."

They stepped into the street to navigate around a crowd of slower moving pedestrians, dodging carriages as they went.

"Who wrote the article?"

"Dr. Ervin Szabó."

The boy nodded, as if this was an important piece of information.

"So he must have mentioned Marx."

"Yes. Karl Marx and Friedrick Engels." She looked at him, hoping for some clarification. "What does it mean if he mentioned Marx?"

"I'm not sure that I can reproduce what they say," Mihály said. "But they have a theory of the way society will evolve, that it will change over time; that with the industrial revolution, which changes society, the proletariat will end up rebelling against the bourgeoisie."

Ella needed to understand this new vocabulary. "What's the proletariat?"

"The workers, more or less."

"Like the peasants?"

"Yes, the peasants perhaps. But I think Marx was thinking of the people who work in factories."

She thought of the Croat couple. The man had come to work in a factory. Was he a proletariat? Proletariat. Where did that word come from? "Like proletarius?"

The boy stopped and stared at her. "You know Latin?"

She smiled and nodded.

"Well, then, socialism comes from the word sociare."

Ella nodded. "To combine or share."

"That's right."

"But it also sounds like society."

"Yes, yes. Maybe it is not that easy."

She felt like she didn't understand at all.

"And what about bourgeoisie? What does bourgeoisie mean?"

"The people who own the means of production. The factory owners."

That would mean Father was a member of the bourgeoisie, which, she supposed meant she was also. Would that mean that his workers would rebel against him?

And where did this boy stand in all this?

She didn't want to tell Mihály she was a member of the bourgeoisie.

"What would I be then? I don't work in a factory or on the land, but I also don't own a factory."

He grinned. "You are a Lady of a Different Sort!"

Ella shook her head. She didn't want to be rude to this

young fellow who was helping her, but she hated his answer. He was dodging her question and it was a serious question.

But she was irritable. She was hungry and tired. She probably wouldn't understand if he tried to explain.

They walked on in silence.

Tante Cecile

Ella and Mihály turned onto a bigger street, with trees planted along the walkway. They passed a little park. A sturdy church stood opposite the park. They crossed the street to a large building with stores on the ground floor.

Mihály opened a door, revealing an elegant lobby. They took the stairs up to the third floor.

Entering the apartment, Mihály led the way to the salon where his mother, a stout woman, slouched on a sofa, smoking a cigarette.

A woman smoking!

Mother said only disreputable women smoked.

Who was this woman? Ella wondered whether she had come to a bad place. A dangerous place. Should she leave?

She probably should, but she was exhausted, too tired to face the bustle of the unknown city below.

"Mutti, this is Ella." Mihály placed his hand on Ella's back nudging her forward. "She is an interesting person. She's run away from home."

With this strange introduction he disappeared.

The woman snuffed out her cigarette in a crystal ashtray, looked at Ella, and spoke in an accented German.

"You've run away from home?"

Ella nodded.

"Are you hungry?"

Ella nodded again.

Mihály's mother called for her maid and asked for a pot of

coffee, rolls and cold cuts.

If this was a bad place, Ella decided, she would figure out how to escape later.

"Thank you, Ma'am."

"Call me Tante Cecile." A gentle smile lit her round face.

"Thank you, Tante Cecile."

Cecile nodded. "I never ran away, but I worried my parents so much they sent me to Vienna."

Her German had a Viennese flavor to it, but also a little something extra.

"That's a little like running away."

The maid set a tray of coffee, cream, and sugar on the table. Cecile poured coffee for Ella and motioned to the cream and sugar.

"Thank you." Ella poured cream into her cup so that the liquid almost spilt over.

"Now that you've run away, what are your plans?"

Ella blushed, thinking of her murky plans.

"I must find some way to support myself...." Mihály's words "women of a certain sort" echoed in her mind. "By tutoring or translating."

"Good, good."

"I can read, write and speak German, French, English, Latin, and, of course, Hungarian."

"Good." Tante Cecile nodded, her gaze focused on Ella. "I know people who could use your talents." A little giggle escaped her lips. "I could use your talents."

The maid set a tray with rolls, butter, jam, and an assortment of meats. Ella eyed the food, but was not going to touch it until it was offered.

"Iss, iss, mein Kind." Cecile pushed the tray toward Ella with her chubby hand. "I bet you haven't had a lot to eat recently."

Ella nodded her thanks, took a roll, broke it open and spread butter on it. She bit into it. It was even better than the café bread. She placed a slice of ham on the roll and took another bite. She closed her eyes relishing the salty flavor of the meat.

"Yes, as I was saying, I can use your talents. My Hungarian is lousy. I need someone to translate for me. All my friends write in those Hungarian journals and I have no idea whether they are brilliant, ignorant or somewhere in between." Cecile poured herself some coffee. "I bet you could translate for me."

Ella gulped. Was it going to be this easy? Did she already have a job? "I'd be happy to, Tante Cecile."

"But there is one fly in the ointment." Her brown eyes stared at Ella. "I can't pay you."

Ella nodded, hoping her voice didn't reveal her disappointment. "I'm good at math. Could I become a bookkeeper?"

She had always been curious about Father's books, but when she had looked at them over his shoulder, he had slammed them shut and said ladies needn't worry about such things.

Tante Cecile rubbed her chin. "Yes, yes. That might work." Again the smile. "I have a friend who's a bookkeeper. She might be able to help you."

Tante heaped sugar into her coffee cup. She was clearly not concerned with her appearance, being both round and rumpled. "You can stay here, with us, until we find something for you."

"Thank you!"

"Yes, yes. You can stay in my daughter Laura's room."

"She won't mind?"

"I don't think so. She's hardly ever here, with her work."

Ella nodded, but her head swirled. Tante's daughter worked. Tante apparently thought it was all right for a woman to work.

But maybe her daughter was an old maid and the family... well, they lived in a nice enough apartment in Budapest, but it was on the third floor, not the second. Maybe Tante needed her daughter to work.

"What kind of work does Laura do?"

"She edits the *International Bibliography of Economics and Sociology*."

"Oh!" Ella wasn't sure what that entailed, but it sounded more glamorous than bookkeeping or translating.

"She just graduated from university."

Ella froze. She had heard from Ede that women in Germany were allowed to attend some lectures, but she didn't know they were allowed to graduate.

"She's my eldest child, my only daughter." Cecile took a cigarette from a silver case and tapped it against the table.

"You will like her, if you ever get a chance to see her."

She flipped a gold lighter open and flicked it. Lighting the cigarette and inhaling, her eyes watered as she blew the acrid smoke into the room.

"By the way, bookkeeper-to-be, how much schooling have you had?"

Ella swallowed, thinking how her education compared to Laura's.

"Just four years at a convent school." She looked at Cecile, waiting for her to decide a bookkeeping job was beyond her reach, but Cecile just nodded. "I know it's not much, and they didn't teach me anything about keeping books, but I received top marks in math." She thought about Zsuzsi. "I did well enough that Sister let me help the other girls."

"Oh, don't look so worried, Ella, my dear." Cecile put her cigarette to her lips and inhaled deeply. "I am sure this will all work out."

166

Ella wondered why Cecile seemed to be so keen to help a girl her son found in a café. Did she always help runaways? But she couldn't ask Cecile that. That would seem ungrateful. She tried another question.

"Why did your father send you to Vienna?"

"He didn't like the company I kept. We lived in Vilna, ruled by the Russians. The Czar was not happy with some of the thoughts floating around, thoughts that I shared. Father feared I would get in trouble with the authorities."

Looking past Ella, Cecile smiled, perhaps thinking back to her Vilna days.

"He was probably right." She inhaled the cigarette again, blowing out little rings of the blue smoke.

"And you, why did you run away from home?"

Ella realized too late it had been a mistake to ask Tante about her past, opening, as it did, a door for her to ask about Ella's situation. She had learned that lying didn't work for her. She wasn't as clever as Huck. Better to be honest and brief.

"I was to be married and I didn't want to be married."

Ella waited for the next question – Why not? – but instead Cecile laughed.

"Good for you!"

Ella held her breath. What kind of lady would congratulate her on running away?

"Good for you!" Tante repeated. "It's time women were allowed to choose their partners. Time for the selling of wives to stop."

Ella stared in disbelief.

"So, I'll stop by my friend Rózsa's and talk to her about bookkeeping. In the meantime, I'll show you where you'll sleep and let you freshen up."

Tante stood, unfolding her short figure and brushing ashes

from her bodice. She turned to the bookcase and removed several journals.

"In the meantime, you can look through these, written in that unfathomable Hungarian of yours." She handed Ella the stack. "Read some article that interests you and we'll talk about it when I come back."

Ella looked down at the publications. *The Twentieth Century* was on top.

Laura

"Ella?"

Ella looked up. A woman, a little older than she, stood at the door, her hand on the door frame.

"Hello, Ella." She approached, offering her outstretched hand. "I'm Mausi."

Ella stood and took her hand, though she was not used to a handshake. "Hello."

"Tilly says that you are going to be staying for a while."

Ella looked down. "I guess."

"It's OK." Mausi chuckled. "It's not the first time we've had guests."

"Oh." Ella wasn't sure who Mausi was, or Tilly, for that matter. "Are you Laura? Tante's daughter?"

She smiled. "Yes, yes. I'm Laura, but everyone calls me Mausi." She shrugged. "Everyone except Mutti, when she is in one of her formal moods."

Ella felt heat rising to her cheeks. She was sitting in Mausi's room. "I took the liberty of...."

"Yes, yes." Mausi eyes scanned Ella's face. "I understand you've had an extraordinary several days."

Ella nodded, not sure what exactly Mausi knew.

"Of course you needed to freshen up." She pulled a chair up to the table. "It's OK. You're welcome here."

Ella swallowed. "Thank you!"

"Of course." Mausi sat down. "Come, show me what you have been reading."

Ella sat down too and flipped the journal to the first page of the article she had been reading.

"This is it, but it is a little difficult for me.

Mausi took the booklet and read a little. "Oh, yes."

"I've heard of socialism before but I don't understand. I don't know lots of the terms...."

Mausi looked up from the article. "Maybe this isn't the best place to start." She ran her finger down several lines. "Ervin assumes you already know a bit."

"Ervin?" The article was written by Dr. Ervin Szabó. Mausi hadn't said Dr. Szabó, she had said Ervin.

Mausi smiled. "Cousin Ervin."

That explained her familiarity, her calling him by his first name, but if 'Ervin" was her cousin, then she must know all this. She must understand it.

"It's OK, Ella. It will all make sense after you think about it. We can talk about it if you like, but right now, I think we should handle some practicalities."

Ella nodded.

"First, you must make yourself at home here, until you get settled." She put her hand on Ella's shoulder. "You are OK here."

Ella swallowed. "But, you... your mother, your brother are all so kind, and you don't know anything about me."

Mausi laughed. "We know quite a bit about you. We know that you are a young woman in trouble. We know that you have run away because you don't want to be married off. We know that you are a curious person, one who wants to understand the world. We know that you are not from Budapest, that you do not know the ways of this city."

Ella bit her lip. "But there must be lots of girls like me...."

"Not so many." Mausi said. "In any case, we are happy to

help."

She stood. "I, in particular, am happy to help. I believe women should be able to create their own destinies, and you are trying to do that. That is brave and deserves encouragement."

She pushed the chair in. "So, let's tour the house first, so you know your way around."

She walked toward the door. Ella followed.

"First stop, the kitchen," Mausi said.

Ella had never toured anyone's house. And starting the tour in the kitchen was strange.

They entered the kitchen, a bit smaller than the kitchen at home. It was equipped with a work table, a sink, an ice box, cabinets full of dishes, all the things a kitchen should have, except for a stove.

Something that looked like a stove stood against the wall, but where did one put the wood to burn? This stove had no belly. And where was the exhaust chimney?

It must be a gas stove. Ella had heard of them, but had never seen one.

The woman who had brought the refreshments to the salon earlier was working at the counter. She looked up.

Mausi placed her hand on Ella's back, gently pushing her forward.

"Tilly, I don't think you've properly met Ella."

Tilly was a broad woman with a wide smile.

"Hello there, Ella!"

Ella tried to smile. She assumed Tilly was the cook, and Tilly had addressed her by her first name! Not as Miss, or Miss Weisel, or even Miss Ella. She had called her Ella.

Tilly would only address her with the familiar Ella if she were Tilly's familiar. What was going on? Did Tilly, like the conductor, think she was a "wench?"

"Tilly cooks and cleans and does all kinds of things," Mausi said. "She's a genius and a magician."

Tilly giggled. "Oh, Mausi...."

Tilly had called Mausi by her first name too!

How strange.

Mausi shook her head. "No, Tilly, it's true." Turning to Ella she said, "If you are hungry, come to Tilly. If you need to know something, come to Tilly."

Ella's smile widened. These people had strange habits, but at least Ella knew she was in the same class, as far as Tilly was concerned, as Mausi. "Thank you!"

"We usually have breakfast at 7. Dinner is usually at 1. And we have tea around 5. Supper is at 8."

Ella nodded.

"If you are going to miss a meal, let Tilly know as soon as possible."

"Yes, of course."

"Thanks, Tilly," Mausi said, walking to the door. "Next stop the salon."

Ella had been in the salon when she had met Tante Cecile, but she had not really looked around, her mind being filled with other thoughts.

The salon had a sofa, overstuffed chairs, two cabinets filled with pictures, figurines, and books, two tables, and straight-back chairs. In Mother's salon, the furniture had set locations, but here the chairs seemed scattered here and there, with no particular place.

Mausi picked up an ashtray that sat on the floor. "Mother's at-home – her salon – is on Saturday, from 2."

In Nagykanizsa people were "at home" at certain times and friends and relatives would come to chat, so Ella was familiar with the idea.

"Outside of that time, this room is usually empty. You can come here to read or write, if you'd like to."

"What's Tante's salon like?"

"You should come and find out. There'll be lots of interesting people. Maybe Ervin will come this Saturday, though I'm not sure if he has left for his holidays."

"Cousin Ervin?" Ella wondered whether she could wear the dress she had on, since she had no other now.

"Yes. You can ask him to explain what he has written." She shrugged her shoulders, "though you shouldn't worry too much about that at the moment."

"Let me show you some other things." Mausi proceeded down the hall, pointing out her parents' bedroom, her father's study, her brothers' room, and her mother's study.

Her mother had a study!

Ella peered in and saw clutter on the desk, books piled, with markers here and there.

"Come, let's sit for a moment." Mausi led Ella back to the salon.

She pulled a key from her pocket, which she gave to Ella.

"The key to the front door. It's best to try to be here before Mutti locks up, about 9 pm, but, in case you aren't here, you have the key. And be forewarned, the building concierge gets grumpy if he has to open the door for you. He usually locks up about 10."

Ella stared at Mausi. "You mean it's OK to be out... out at night."

"Well, I wouldn't go out by myself at night. But yes, it's OK."

"Is it OK to be out by myself, during the day?"

Mausi chuckled. "Good question. I'll find a map, so we can talk about places to avoid."

She pulled a watch from her pocket, frowning as she looked at it. "But, I'm running late. I need to get back to work."

Work! Yes, Ella remembered. Mausi worked.

Ella wanted to know what an editor did. Mausi's life seemed charmed. She was educated. She had the kind of work Ella thought she wanted. She was elegant, not in Mother's fashion, but in a sensible way, wearing comfortable but perfectly tailored clothes.

"A couple of other things. Mutti isn't very practical, so if you have questions, ask me or Tilly."

Ella wondered whether 'Mutti' would agree, but she just nodded.

"Make yourself comfortable. I won't be home much, so you can spread out in our room."

Ella nodded again.

"I won't be back for supper, but you'll meet my brothers."

Ella nodded. "Thank you."

Mausi stood and started to the door. She turned to look at Ella.

"And relax. It will all be all right."

It will be All Right

Ella sat, thinking about all Mausi had said.

A key to the house! She could come and go as she pleased.

Tell Tilly if she didn't plan to be home for dinner!

In Nagykanizsa, Mother planned her days, when she would meet whom and for how long. It was Ella who was informed what would be happening, usually just before it happened.

And Mausi, so efficient and elegant. How was that possible?

It seemed a contradiction, but Mausi seemed forbidding. She smiled and said everything would be all right, that Ella should make herself at home. But somehow Ella didn't believe it.

Maybe it was her efficiency. She had things that needed to be done. Tell Ella the ways of the house, make sure she had a key, answer questions, and when those things were done, as if she had a checklist, then she left.

She was efficient but less warm, less kind than her brother Mihály.

And she wasn't curious. She didn't ask where Ella was from or why she had run away or what she would like to do. It was as if all those questions had already been answered or, if not, she wasn't interested.

Mausi was just doing her job, for this particular runaway. She said that they had had guests before. Maybe this was part of her job, to handle the runaways. Maybe this was a job she didn't really like, but one that had to be done.

And the comment about her mother: "Mutti isn't very practical." But it was Tante who said she could find Ella work and that was what she wanted more than anything else. Work. Mausi hadn't said anything about finding work.

Ella yawned. It had been, as Mausi said, an extraordinary day. She wondered what Ede was doing. Did he know by now that she had left? Was he angry? Or sad? Would he turn into the tyrant Mother had described and come for her?

Who was Ede?

She had never thought of Ede as a tyrant. Or Father, for that matter. Father could be blunt with Mother, but that seemed necessary.

Should she believe what Mother said about men?

She couldn't picture Father hurting anyone, let alone his bride on their wedding night.

Was this Mother's final revenge, to poison her marriage to Ede?

That didn't seem possible.

Mother was difficult, but not cunning. That was too subtle for Mother.

No, not revenge.

But mad? Was her mother crazy? Had she lost her mind when her Erzsébet died?

That seemed more probable.

What difference did it make? There was no going back. Anyway, she didn't want to go back. Ella sighed.

By now all of Nagykanizsa would know that she took the train to Budapest. Mr. Kovacs probably told everyone who wandered into the station. She imagined one of his drinking buddies stopping by and Mr. Kovacs telling him. The buddy would go down to the tavern and tell everyone there. Then one of the waiters would tell everyone in the tavern kitchen, and one of the dishwashers would run to tell her sweetheart. It was all over town by now.

And what about Mother?

Ella wouldn't have been at the breakfast table and Mother would have gone to her room to find out why. She would have discovered the note and then what? She would show it to Father.

Would they come after her? Or send Miklos? Or tell Ede and ask him to go after her? Or maybe Mother would have simply fainted, unable to cope with another disgrace.

And what if Miklos came for her? Budapest was a big city. He would never find her here, would he?

And what about Ede?

A pang stung her heart. She had disgraced her family, and she didn't care about that. But she had disgraced Ede. Everyone knew they were to be married and she had run away.

What would people think? She wished she had not left. She wished she had talked to him. They had always talked. But she wasn't sure she could tell him. She didn't trust him. But if she didn't trust him, who could she trust?

Oh Ede!

But she couldn't go back to Nagykanizsa. She could write to him. She would say... what could she say? I'm sorry! She was very, very sorry. But was that enough?

It was not enough. She could never make it up to him.

It would never be all right.

This is what she had chosen. She hoped Tante would find her a job. She would make enough money to go to Vienna.

She must forget about Ede. She had done horrible harm, but she couldn't undo it. She must look to the future and forget him.

She remembered his kiss. She remembered the warmth of his body as he embraced her, his finger tracing the line of her cheek.

"Ella?"

She opened her eyes. It was Tante's hand on her cheek.

"Come, it's time for supper." Tante offered her hand.

Ella took her hand and stood.

"I have wonderful news for you!" Tante said, putting her hand on Ella's shoulder. "Rózsa thinks she can find work for you as a bookkeeper's assistant." She was guiding Ella toward the dining room. "And she can help you study to take your exams."

"Exams?"

"Yes, yes." Tante said as she entered the dining room. "We will talk about that later. But now you must meet my sons and we must have supper.

Tante rushed through the introductions. Adolf was the oldest son, maybe a few years older than Ella, Karl, the middle son was about her age, and finally Mihály.

Tilly set a platter of cold cuts and cheeses on the table as soon as Tante and Ella sat down.

"Where's Mausi?" Adolf said, as he broke a roll.

"She's never home," Mihály said.

Adolf buttered his roll and took a bite. "Ever since she graduated from university, she seems to have better things to do than be with us."

Ella stared at Adolf.

"Now, now," Tante set her cup down. "She's busy with her work. The bibliography is due out soon and now that Ervin isn't working on it, it's all on her shoulders."

Karl sipped his coffee. "I think she has a new beau."

Tante raised her eyebrows. "Who?"

Karl grinned and shrugged.

Rózsa and Suska

Ella should be pleased. This world, this strange Budapest, with its educated women, women who had jobs and were allowed to find their own beaus, she knew this should be her paradise. But she had no time to contemplate such incredible possibilities. Tante Cecile was rushing her.

"Rózsa will see you this morning, just as soon as we can get to her office. We must hurry."

They walked into the June morning, already warm, Tante Cecile talking in streams.

"Rózsa is moody, but don't let that put you off. You don't need to work with her forever, just make a good impression. Tell her you want to work."

Tante hailed a coach. It stopped and they climbed in.

"And tell her that you have English. She may be able to use that. Some businesses need someone who has English. And of course French and German, but English might be more important."

Ella tried to get a sense of the direction they were going as they traveled away from the river and a little north.

Tante's instructions continued.

"Don't say much other than that. Rózsa likes to argue, but never mind. Just don't disagree."

Tante looked out the window and pointed. "That's where Laura works."

Ella tried to determine which building it was, but Tante's conversation turned back to Rózsa.

"She will probably try your languages, so be prepared."

Tante rubbed her chin, her forehead furrowed. "You might mention Latin too, since all the old laws were in Latin." She shrugged. "I mean, maybe that will help in getting you work, but maybe it will help in other ways."

Tante was making Ella nervous. This Rózsa sounded formidable. But she reminded herself how kind, how thoughtful Tante was, trying to help her. How fortunate she had been to have found her.

Perhaps fate was on her side, having placed her in the hands of this woman, a woman like no other she had ever met.

The coach stopped, Tante paid the driver and they turned to the building, tall and squeezed on either side by equally tall buildings. They entered and climbed the stairs.

Rózsa's office was cramped. Books and papers were scattered on every horizontal surface. Two women sat at a table going over notes. The shorter, rounder one stood. "Ah, Cecile, I see you brought your new friend."

"Yes, Rózsa, this is Ella." Tante looked at Ella, who stepped forward.

Rózsa eyed Ella, from her head to her shoes, then glared. "And do you have a last name, Ella?"

Ella remained resolved to just tell the truth. "Yes, ma'am, Ella Weisel"

"No, no." Rózsa shook her head. "No formalities here. It's Rózsa."

Ella added this to her list of Budapest's absurdities. No formal titles, just Rózsa. "Yes, Rózsa."

"Of course, at work we must follow the old ways and use the titles. But among ourselves, that is different."

Ella inhaled the musty book scent of the room, like her father's study, but missing the tobacco and mint. "Yes, M...

Rózsa."

"And you want to be a bookkeeper?"

"Yes. Or anything else I might do. I have English, French, and Latin, as well as Hungarian and German, of course."

"Really?" For the first time Rózsa's eyes shone. "Just speaking? Or can you also read and write them?"

"Read and write."

"How can that be?" The intense gray eyes held Ella's. "With only four years at a convent school?"

"My parents had French tutors for us. For a while." Too short a while Ella remembered, "I had a governess from Chicago."

Rózsa's eyes widened. "From Chicago?"

Ella smiled, thinking of Alexa. "Yes, yes. Her English was perfect. American English, of course. But she went back to Chicago to get married."

"I see." Rózsa's rubbed her fingers on her cheek. "And Latin?"

"My friend. He taught me Latin."

"He?"

Ella felt her cheeks burn.

"Yes." She forced a little smile. "He was, well, sort of a member of the family."

She felt the weight of the pendant under her blouse. This strange woman didn't need to know more than this.

Rózsa switched to English. "I see. Well, never mind. I can only get you an assistant position, for little pay. You will need to study for exams, but I have the books here. I assume that you can do that."

Ella shifted her weight from one foot to the other. She responded in English. "Yes. Of course."

In French Rózsa said. "I expect you to start studying immediately."

"Oui. Immediately."

And in Hungarian Rózsa said, "And, as a price for my finding you employment, I expect you to help us here."

"Igen."

Ella wasn't sure what kind of help would be expected of her, but right now this seemed her best opportunity.

"I will be happy to help."

Rózsa looked down at the other woman still sorting papers at the table.

"Suska will give you some materials to study."

Apparently this was as much of an introduction Suska was going to get. She stood. Her face was round, her eyes kind. She had a pleasant, if a little plump, figure. She was poised and older than Ella, but not by much. Ella felt immediately drawn to her, perhaps because she seemed reserved, not quite as assertive as the other women.

"Give her the first-year text for bookkeeping," Rózsa said, "And give her some pamphlets. Let's try English first. And give her a notebook."

Suska nodded at Rózsa and turned to Ella. "Come. Let's see what we can find."

They went to the bookcase in the next room and Suska pulled a thick book from one shelf and several pamphlets from another. She gathered a blank notebook from the top of the cabinet.

When they returned, Rózsa's voice was raised, and Cecile was smiling but shaking her head. Perhaps, Ella thought, Rózsa was not the only one who liked to argue.

Rózsa focused on Ella. "I will see you day after tomorrow. I want one of those pamphlets translated."

Ella's heart leaped, she wanted to dance. She could not imagine work she would rather do.

"Yes. To German or Hungarian?"

"Hungarian." She looked around the room. "When you come again, you will spend the day here. Can you type?"

Ella shook her head.

Rózsa nodded towards a table in the corner, just big enough to hold the typewriter that sat on it, with a little space left for papers.

"If we don't have work for you by then, you will start to learn to type."

Ella knew that Ede had paid to get his thesis typed. She eyed the typewriter, unsure how she felt about typing. Would she be as clumsy at it as she had been at tatting? Never mind. Right now she had few options.

"Yes, Rózsa."

"Now, Suska and I have some things to do," Rózsa said.

Without further ceremony, Rózsa sat at the table and looked expectantly at Suska, who smiled at Ella.

"Good to meet you, Ella." Her gaze turned to Tante Cecile. "Nice to see you, Cecile. Have a nice afternoon."

They descended the stairs from the office and walked into the noon heat.

"We need to get home for dinner." Tante said. She hailed a coach and they settled in the compartment.

"So, my Ella, I think you impressed Rózsa."

Ella gulped. "I hope so."

"You passed the first language tests."

Ella exhaled, trying to release the tension in her jaw.

"Now, do a good job on the translation!"

Ella closed her eyes. She had never doubted her abilities before, but now? Translating a whole pamphlet? She had never done that before.

"Tante, do you have an English-Hungarian dictionary?"

"Possibly. Ask Mausi."

Mausi was not at dinner, so she asked Karl, who produced a small one from his room. Ella longed for the one Ede had, much larger, but she would have to do with what she had.

She flipped through the pamphlets as she lay on her bed. She chose one called "*Fruits of Philosophy*" because it seemed to be shorter and the font was large and clear. She read the subtitle, "A Treatise on the Population Question."

Fruits of Philosophy

After breakfast the next morning, Ella settled at the writing table in the salon. She opened the blank notebook and laid a pen and an ink bottle beside it. Opening the pamphlet *"Fruits of Philosophy,"* she leaned back in the chair. She had skimmed through the booklet yesterday. Today she would read it more carefully and then translate.

The first heading read "Philosophical Proem." She had never heard or seen the word "proem" and it was not in Karl's little dictionary. She rubbed her hands together, clammy despite the warmth of the June morning. She looked over the two pages, skimming, words skittering here and there. "Senses," "appetites," "happiness," "sin."

What did all this have to do with bookkeeping? Why would Rózsa be interested in this essay? Then her eye rested on the words "productive instinct." Was this the desire to work? That could not be, because the entire sentence was:

> *"Man by nature is endowed with the talent of devising means to remedy or prevent the evils that are liable to arise from gratifying our appetites; and it is as much the duty of the physician to inform mankind of the means to prevent the evils that are liable to arise from gratifying the productive instinct as it is to inform them how to keep clear of the gout or dyspepsia."*

Ella could not imagine the "evils that are liable to arise" from the desire to work. "Gratifying the productive instinct" had to be... Ella saw the mare's outstretched neck. This essay must be about the means to prevent the evils from satisfying sexual desire.

Her eyes scanned down to the next heading "Chapter 1: To Limit at Will the Number of Their Offspring."

"Showing how desirable it is, both in a political and a social point of view, for mankind to be able to limit at WILL THE NUMBER OF THEIR OFFSPRING, WITHOUT SACRIFICING THE PLEASURE THAT ATTENDS THE GRATIFICATION OF THE REPRODUCTIVE INSTINCT."

Ella swallowed. The next section was about politics. She skipped it. The next section discussed the social aspects of the problem:

Is it not notorious that the families of the married often increase beyond which a regard for the young beings coming into the world, and the happiness of those who give them birth, would dictate? In how many instances does the hard-working father, and more especially the mother, of a poor family remain slave throughout their lives, tugging at the oar of incessant labor, toiling to live, and living to toil; when, if their offspring had been limited to two or three only, they might have enjoyed comfort and comparative affluence?

This pamphlet might have, at least in part, a solution to the dilemma her mother complained of: being sick with child. Having one child after another.

She read further. It reminded her of Ede's essay on the sorrows of sex.

The next section was labeled "On Generation." It was a

detailed description of the female reproductive organs. Ella was not sure she understood and wondered whether she wanted to translate it, it seeming somehow sinful.

No.

Of course she could.

The author had said that knowledge should not be kept from people, and she would not keep this knowledge secret just because... she gulped... it seemed prurient, something that ought not to be talked about.

She felt restless as she read about the anatomical details and her eyes slid over the words to the next chapter: "On Promoting and Checking Conception."

Checking conception.

That was what she had asked Ede about and he had assured her that there were methods of making sure she did not become pregnant, even though they had... well, they were man and wife.

She skimmed the paragraphs on promoting conception, trying to find the information about checking it.

There it was.

She read quickly, feeling her heart beating. She did not understand the words: semen, vagina, baudruche. She didn't understand what was being said. The author was recommending some methods, noting that others were probably not so good.

Ella closed her eyes.

Should she believe these things?

The author seemed to be a doctor.

She went back to the beginning of the document. There it was. It was written by Charles Knowlton, M. D., medical doctor.

So Ede was right. There were ways to prevent pregnancies.

How could she have doubted him?

Oh Ede!

She felt so sorry. She longed to see him. To fall into his arms. To inhale his scent and feel his embrace.

That was not to be.

She chose this new life. So be it. There was no going back, no matter how she wished for it.

She would not think about Ede.

She read the entire pamphlet, straight through. At the back of the notebook, she made a list of the words she did not know how to translate. She read the pamphlet through again. She managed to eliminate several of the words, having understood the good doctor's anatomy lesson.

She started on her translation, writing as neatly as she could. Once she had pushed aside her doubts, she quite enjoyed the project.

"Ella?"

Mausi stood at the door. "It's time for dinner."

"Oh. Sorry." Ella stacked her papers, set them to the side, and followed Mausi to the dining room.

In addition to Tante, Adolf, Karl, and Mihály, an older gentleman sat at the head of the table. He nodded to her, pushing back from the table, rising and offering his hand. "Call me Onkel Mihály, Ella."

"Yes... Onkel Mihály." She shook his hand.

"I hear you are deep in a translation project," Onkel Mihály said as he resettled at the table.

Ella took her seat. "Yes, Onkel."

"And what are you translating?"

All eyes were on her. "It's called *'Fruits of Philosophy'*."

"What's it about?" Adolf smiled.

Ella felt her cheeks burn.

"It's a famous pamphlet." Mausi laughed. "Outlawed first in the United States and then in Britain."

Onkel frowned. "So, are we having Ella translate something that will get her arrested?"

"Oh, I don't think so." Tante Cecile took a sip of her wine. "The emperor is too busy with other problems."

"Other problems? Like the rioting peasants?" Adolf shook his head. "Who cares about the emperor and his problems? What is this pamphlet about and why would it be outlawed?"

Mausi sighed. "It details methods of contraception, obscene contraception, and is therefore considered illegal."

So that was what preventing pregnancies was called: contraception. It made sense contra – against – ception – conceiving.

"Still?" Mihály sat up and shook his head. "Is discussion of contraception still considered obscene?"

"I'm not sure if it is still considered illegal." Mausi smiled. "Which is too bad, since every time someone was brought to trial for writing or publishing the paper, the pamphlet's circulation increased." She patted her lips with her napkin. "It was a wonderful way to educate women about contraception, a wonderful way to teach young women things they should know."

Rózsa again

Ella woke from a dream featuring the man with sour breath, her sheet in a tangle, her face sweaty. She slowly reconstructed her situation: she was at Tante's house and today she was to see Rózsa again.

This didn't calm her.

She had translated only the "Proem," whatever that meant, and the first chapter. And she had a long list of words she didn't know and weren't in Karl's dictionary. If only she had spent less time reading about the prevention of conception.

She sat at the breakfast table, her stomach churning. She sipped her coffee and pulled a bit of crust from her roll.

Tante pushed her plate to the side and lit a cigarette. "I have a meeting this morning." She exhaled blue smoke rings. "Important meeting, about my article for the *Neues Pester Journal*."

"Tante?" Under the table Ella dug her finger nails into her palm. "Was I to meet with Rózsa today?"

"Yes, yes," Tante put her cigarette to her lips and inhaled. "Yes. You can walk."

Ella gulped as Tante disappeared out the door.

Mausi shook her head and laughed. "Mutti, Mutti!" She turned to Ella. "Don't look so worried. I'll draw you a map."

Last night's dream of sour breath swept through Ella's mind. She felt the streets might be unsafe, even though she had walked from the train station into Pest without trouble.

"Is it safe for me to walk by myself?"

"Just follow the route I give you and you'll be fine," Mausi said.

Ella brought paper and pencil. Mausi described the route as she drew the map.

"Head east, away from the Danube," She drew several wavy lines and a fish to show the Danube.

"That's Kossuth Lajos út, but it changes names to Rákóczi út. Turn right here." Laura continued, writing down the street names and drawing the path.

Ella tried to memorize the route. If it had been in Nagykanizsa, it would have been easy. But here she didn't know the street names and she didn't know any of the landmarks.

"How long will it take me?"

"Maybe half an hour." Laura handed the map to Ella.

"And pay no attention to anyone along the way. Just walk, as if you were in a hurry, keep your gaze ahead." Laura smiled at her. "No one will bother you if you seem to be rushed."

Ella nodded.

"I've got to be off." At the door Mausi turned to Ella. "Good luck with Mrs. Mercurial."

Mrs. Mercurial. That must be Rózsa.

Ella went to their room, washed up and brushed her hair, pinning it up in a loose bun. She smoothed her skirt. She had only brought the clothes she was wearing. They would have to do, even though her blouse was wrinkled and tired, her skirt not much better.

Gathering her things, she looked at the map again, trying to remember all the directions. Looking at it when she was walking would be a sure sign she was a stranger and therefore a target. She shoved the paper into her pocket.

It was already hot even though it was early. She walked the

route, paying attention to the street signs, until she found a turn she must take. She made the turn and consulted the map again, then continued walking.

By the time she had reached Rózsa's door she was sweaty and tired, and nervous too because she had not translated the entire pamphlet.

She knocked timidly on the door.

Rózsa opened the door and examined her through wire rim glasses, which accentuated the darkness under her eyes.

"Well, at last!" She turned to one side to let Ella enter. "I thought you decided not to come."

"No, Mrs. Schwimmer, I had to walk because Tante had an important meeting."

"Rózsa. Call me Rózsa!"

Ella should've remembered this request. She'd made a bad impression just by saying hello.

"Yes Rózsa." Ella looked around the little room, disappointed not to see Suska there.

Rózsa sat at the table and reached for the documents.

"Well, let me see what you have."

Ella handed her the notebook.

"I only translated the first two parts." She perched on the chair opposite Rózsa.

Rózsa was already reading. Her frown deepened as she nodded.

"I see."

Ella felt like she had to defend herself.

"I had only a small dictionary."

Rózsa's finger ran down the page as she read.

"Where's the pamphlet?"

Ella handed her the booklet.

Rózsa opened it looking back and forth between it and the

translation.

Ella sat, watching the woman read, turn pages back and forth. She slid her hand in her pocket and fingered the map.

At last Rózsa looked up. "I think you will not be a bookkeeper."

Ella held her breath, not certain what that meant.

"You will tutor children in English." Rózsa didn't seem to like this particular decision. Her eyes were hard and her mouth a thin disapproving line.

"Give me the bookkeeping lessons. I will need them for someone else."

Ella had been so concerned with the translation, she had not thought about the book and had not brought it.

"I left the bookkeeping lessons at Tante's."

"Well, you need to bring it back." The woman stared at Ella over her glasses. "Today."

"Yes, M... Rózsa."

"Go get it now."

"Yes, Rózsa."

The older woman handed the pamphlet and the notebook back to Ella.

"And complete the translation."

"Do you have a better dictionary?"

"Yes, of course."

Rózsa stood, her short stout figure looming.

"Get the book. When you return you can consult the dictionary."

As the door closed, none too gently behind her, Ella exhaled.

She would be tutoring.

Maybe bookkeeping would be better. Maybe one could make more money. And she would have learned about business. She had wanted to learn about business.

But tutoring…she could handle that.

Besides, beggars could not be choosers.

She put her hand in her pocket.

The map was not there!

It must have slipped from her pocket when she was with Rózsa.

Should she go back to retrieve it?

What would Rózsa think of her?

No.

She could remember the way back. It wasn't that far.

And she didn't want Rózsa to think she was a fool.

She started down the street, making a left turn at the corner, since she had turned right on her way to Rózsa's. She looked around her, realizing that this morning she had concentrated on the street names, so she hadn't noticed landmarks.

It all looked busy, big, and confusing.

Never mind. She remembered the name of the next street, St. Stephen's út. She thought she needed to turn right.

The next street was called Rákóczi út. She watched the street signs as she walked.

The day had grown hotter and she felt perspiration on her chest, under her arms, on her face. She walked on.

No Rákóczi út.

Had she missed it?

She looked up and down the street, wishing she had paid more attention to her surroundings.

She continued walking, wondering whether she should have turned right instead of left.

Again she stopped. The buildings looked shabby, the street narrower than the streets she had traveled before.

She wrinkled her nose at the faint smell of stewed cabbage and urine.

Ruined Plans

Ella looked around. She had to find someone who could help her get back to Tante Cecile's.

A man walking in the opposite direction, a man with a ragged jacket and scuffed shoes, eyed Ella.

She hurried past him.

If Ella could find a shop, she could ask.

She tried to remember Tante's address.

The lost map had the name of every street she had to use, but not the street she started from. Maybe she could describe the street with the park and the sturdy church. Perhaps they would recognize Tante's last name, Polanyi. Or her full name, or that of Mr. Polanyi, or one of their children.

It was a slim chance, but still, she had to try.

She walked by a butcher shop. A man with a dark face stood behind the counter, the only person in the store.

Ella passed by.

The next store sold vegetables. Again the shop keeper was a man, a young man with unruly hair. But here, at least, several customers, woman customers, were shopping.

As she took the handle of the door, she felt an arm reach over her shoulder and across her chest.

A strong meaty hand shoved her hand almost to her shoulder blade. A ragged pain shot through her body.

The pamphlet and notebook fell to the ground.

She tried to swing her other hand behind her, but it flayed uselessly in the air.

The grasp across her chest tightened so that the emerald necklace cut into her collarbone.

"Do as I say, so I do not need to hurt you further." The voice was deep, and though it was but a whisper, it was commanding.

Ella arched her back and kicked her right leg up and back.

Her shoulder popped as her hand was pushed farther up her back.

"Nice spirit, little filly. Now behave."

Ella's throat tightened as she tried to scream. A pitiful little "ah" emerged from her lips.

"I don't want to damage my goods, filly, so for both of us, behave."

She felt perspiration run down her face. Her shoulder burned. She gasped.

The pressure on her chest restricted her lungs, and as she tried to pull in air, a shot of pain, like hot metal, raced through her shoulder.

The door in front of her melted as darkness descended.

When Ella awoke, a face with wrinkled brows and a mole, just where her mother's mole was, met her eyes.

Ella blinked.

It was Aunt Ilona's face.

Aunt Ilona smiled as she wiped a cool cloth across Ella's brow. "Miklos! Miklos!"

Ella tried to sit up, but her left arm was weak, useless, the shoulder bound. She fell back to the bed.

She saw Miklos' dark face, his mustache long. He stared down on her from over Aunt Ilona's shoulder.

"You idiot!"

"Miklos, darling. Not now. Her shoulder, the doctor said it should get better."

196

Miklos' deep voice flooded the room. "Now. She needs to hear this now."

"Doctor gave her morphine for the pain." Aunt's lips pressed tight. "You'll frighten her."

Miklos's furious face focused on his aunt and his voice boomed. "Good! That's what I want to do."

"Miklos, please!"

"Aunt." Miklos continued staring at the old woman. "Go."

He started to pull her, but she obeyed, standing up. She hesitated. Miklos reached to shove her toward the door.

"Now."

Aunt Ilona lowered her head and walked quickly to the door, her handkerchief at her eyes.

Miklos turned back to his sister.

"You idiot!" He stood over her, glaring at her. "Why did you leave?"

"I...." Ella's throat was sore. She cleared it. "I...."

Not waiting for her response, Miklos broke in. "You had everything! Ede is...." Miklos shook his head. "He should be outraged, but he is somewhere in the city, looking for you."

Ella winced. Her chest stung under the pendant.

"The idiot still wants to marry you."

Ella stared at Miklos. Her mother's words "had his way with me" raced through her mind.

"And if you have half a brain, you will marry and be a dutiful wife."

Ella closed her eyes. Why was she with Aunt Ilona? She remembered coming to Budapest, but how did she get here?

He snorted. "I can see you are unconvinced. Let me explain the facts of life to you, little Virgin Mary."

He touched her shoulder. A shot of pain surged. She whimpered as she opened her eyes.

What had happened to her?

Miklos' voice was hoarse and gravelly. "Good. Look at me. And listen."

He was silent, but she said nothing.

She remembered trying to find her way back to Tante's.

She remembered the arm across her chest.

She remembered her hand shoved up her back and the sound of tearing at her shoulder.

Miklos' voice pierced her thoughts. "Do you understand what could have happened if our detective hadn't found you?"

"Your detective?"

She leaned on her right side and pushed herself up, ignoring the acidy reflux in her throat.

"You hired that... that...?" Her heart pounded, she expelled a deep breath, her voice jagged. "Thug!"

"Yes!" His lips curled in an unkind smile. "Yes."

He slowly nodded, as if this confirmed the justification of his actions. "A damned good thing we did, too. He said he found you in an unsavory part of Pest."

He had used the word we. Did that mean... "You and Ede hired that...."

"Yes, of course." He shook his head. "Though I am not sure I would have been so kind if I were Ede."

She swallowed. She could understand Miklos hiring such a ruffian. But Ede? Was that like Ede?

Never mind, she wasn't going to marry Ede. She was going to get a job and support herself. She was going to be an English tutor. Rózsa said she was going to be....

"Oh!" Her right hand covered her mouth. "I was supposed to get the book for Rózsa... and Tilly would have expected...."

Miklos interrupted. "Never mind what silly thing you thought you were going to do." His words, sharp and cutting, came rapidly. "If our man had not found you, someone could have abducted you."

"No!" She had gotten to Budapest without trouble. Well, there was Sour Breath, but she had managed that.

"If you were very lucky, he would have only stolen whatever you had."

She shook her head.

"If you were only lucky, he would have raped you."

Miklos looked at her, spit flying from his mouth, as he annunciated each word.

"Rape, Virgin Mary. Do you know the word rape?"

Miklos spit out "Virgin Mary" with scorn, as he always did.

"He would have disrobed you and forced his penis into you."

She thought of her mother, what she had said about Father. She thought of Sour Breath.

"He might have beaten you, or tortured you, or killed you."

Maybe Miklos was right. She didn't want to admit it, but she did not prevent his thug from taking her.

He frowned. "And that would not have been the worst of it."

She swallowed.

"He might have impregnated you. You understand? A child might have been conceived."

Ella saw Therese's body on the bed, the red strain spreading.

"Or he might have given you a disease, like syphilis."

"Syphilis?"

"Yes, you fool, syphilis. A disease that will kill you, but only after it has tortured you."

She felt exhausted and leaned back on the pillows.

"Or, it is possible that he would have given you both gifts: a child and syphilis."

He had made his point. She just wanted him to leave.

"Worse yet, he might have sold you to a brothel or rented you out to men who want sex or sent you to Turkey or Russia, where they especially like Hungarian women."

She remembered the thug's words, "don't damage my goods."

"Good. I can see you're frightened."

She was.

She needed to learn the city. She would learn the rules from Mausi, if only she could find her way back to Tante's.

"Now that I have educated you, curious Virgin Mary, you understand me."

She nodded, because if she agreed perhaps he would leave her. She needed to be well and get back to Tante's.

"Thank Mother for protecting you all these years."

"No!" She would not thank Mother.

"Very well. Marry that fool Ede, who still wants you. Marry him, obey him, and thank him every day."

She wouldn't marry Ede, but no point in arguing.

"Or, if my Virgin Mary is too good to marry him, let Father put you in a convent."

She expelled a bitter chuckle.

"Now, I have to find Ede, who is out combing Budapest for you."

He turned on his heel and left.

Ella stared, seeing nothing. Was she lucky?

No.

If Miklos and Ede had left her alone, if that thug had not kidnapped her, she would have found her way back to Tante Cecile's.

She grasped the lock of hair at her right ear, sliding the strands between her fingers.

She was just about to find work, to support herself, to be

independent.

But now what? What must Rózsa think? What must Tante Cecile think? She had to get up and find them.

As she tried to push herself up, her stomach churned and the room spun before her. She gasped, unable to fill her lungs. She fell back to the pillows.

Ede's Question

Aunt Ilona instructed Flora, her cook, to set the full tray on the table.

"You need to eat and drink, my girl."

Aunt Ilona poured a cup of tea, placed a bed tray over Ella's lap, and handed the tea to her. She pulled up a chair and settled by the bed.

"Thank you." Ella placed the tea on the tray.

"What's that?" Ilona held an ear trumpet to her ear and turned her head, so that Ella was staring at the instrument's shiny metal.

Ella smiled. "Thank you, Aunt Ilona."

Her aunt put the instrument down and beamed at Ella. "What I can't understand is why you didn't tell me you were coming. I'd have met you at the station or sent someone to fetch you."

Again Ella was confronted with the ear horn. "I should have done that."

No reason not to agree with her agreeable aunt. She clearly didn't understand the situation. It was a relief to be with her, someone who just wanted to be kind and helpful.

"Yes, yes." Aunt nodded. "And poor Ede was so upset you weren't here. He and Miklos came right here looking for you."

Ella nodded again. That seemed easier than trying to make her aunt hear her. Or trying to explain the situation to her, if she could explain the situation.

What was she going to do?

"Ede seems like such a nice man. You are so lucky to be marrying him."

Ella nodded and smiled. No need to try to explain that she wasn't going to marry him. She wouldn't explain yet. Not until she could get out of bed and find Tante Cecile and Rózsa. She was feeling better. She was sitting up. Did she dare try to get out of bed?

"You need to eat." Ilona dished food onto a plate. "Some sausage. Bread. And a little fruit."

She placed the full plate on the bed tray, which Ella managed, with difficulty, to keep balanced.

"Flora got these raspberries at market today. Very good, I think."

Ilona settled back in her chair.

Ella took in a good breath and yelled. "Thank you!"

She wondered whether she could eat, whether her stomach had settled enough to keep food down.

Ilona smiled and nodded. "That Ede. Very handsome. Such a lucky girl!"

Ede was handsome. Ella felt like she was lying, not correcting her aunt's understanding of the situation. But right now she needed to think. She needed to be well.

She nibbled at the bread and discovered she was hungry. She took a bite of sausage, relishing its tang. She was better!

"I am hungry!"

"Good."

"How have you been, Aunt?"

"Oh, the knees hurt. And the back." She shrugged. "The wages of living too long."

Ella nodded as the sweet-tart flavor of a raspberry filled her mouth.

Ilona sighed. "But the good lord will take me when He is

ready."

Mischief twinkled in her eyes, but then, as if she would only allow herself so much fun at God's expense, she crossed herself.

The door swung open banging into the wall. Ede stood in the doorway, his face dark, his eyes set on Ella.

"You are here." He strode forward. "Thank God!"

"Ede!" Ilona rose, offering the chair to him. "You will want to talk to your bride."

She disappeared, closing the door behind her.

Ede stood behind the chair, leaning on its back, looking down on Ella.

"Why?" He shook his head. "Why did you leave?"

She did not want to answer that.

"I went off with your necklace. But I have it." She touched the stone's facets. "I just can't take it off, with my arm...."

He blinked. "Never mind the necklace."

Were those tears gathering?

"I will never find another woman whose eyes match that stone. It's yours, just as I...."

He turned his head so she could no longer see his face, shuddering as he exhaled.

He looked back at her with hard eyes. "Never mind the necklace. It is yours. Someday you may need it."

His voice was louder now, more insistent. "Why did you leave?"

She shook her head. "Is it true what Miklos says?"

She didn't want to tell him why she left. She didn't want him to be here. She wanted to escape back to before the detective had ruined her plans.

"What does he say?"

Better this topic, she supposed.

"That I was lucky that I wasn't raped or beaten or sold to a brothel or taken to Russia like a pet dog."

"Yes." He pursed his lips. "Yes, you were lucky."

He leaned farther down. "Why did you leave?"

She was not going to answer that question. She tried to tap into his crusade, his desire for a better Hungary. "How can we live in such a world?"

A smile came to his lips, almost a sneer really.

"Yes, my darling. How can we?"

His face grew even darker.

"Right now, however, the only thing I must know is why you left."

She shook her head. "I cannot tell you."

"Ella, Ella." He pulled the chair behind him and sat. His voice turned mellow. "You can tell me anything. We have always told each other everything."

His gentler gaze warmed her heart. But no, she would not explain. Better that he be angry. Better that he think she didn't love him.

"I decided that I didn't want to marry."

His face whitened.

Ella wondered at herself. How could she be so cruel? "Ever."

His eyes were blank.

"I don't want to marry. Anyone. Ever."

She wasn't lying.

Not exactly.

That was not the reason she left. But it was true that she had decided not to marry.

He stood abruptly, the chair falling behind him with a clatter. He didn't seem to notice, but stomped through the door, slamming it behind him.

The stillness of the room filled Ella. She sobbed. She didn't know why she was crying.

She must not cry.

She must get better and find Rózsa and Tante Cecile.

Miklos Reconsiders

Ella woke to the sound of footsteps. The moon shone in the window and her brother's silhouette paced back and forth across the room.

"Miklos?"

"Ah, you're awake." His tone was softer than during his outburst of the afternoon. "I hope I didn't wake you, but I need to talk to you."

She tried to sit up, but a streak of pain rushed through her shoulder when she put weight on her left hand. She collapsed back.

"What time is it?"

"Just after midnight." He stood at the bed and looked down on her. "I was frantic earlier."

She pushed herself to a sitting position with her feet and her right arm.

"It's OK." She stared at his lined face. He seemed ten years older. "Are you all right?"

As he exhaled, his body seemed smaller, vulnerable. He shook his head.

"So much has happened and I lose my good sense." He sank to the bed. "I probably shouldn't have said all those things to you."

"Perhaps."

She was still perturbed. She would have found her way to Tante's. But she also wanted a clear view of the world and he had educated her.

"I needed to know."

He smiled. "Yes, you would say that, my dear sister." He chuckled. "My dear, curious sister."

"But it's true!"

She thought of Sour Breath. She now understood why young women did not travel alone. If someone had explained that to her, she would have.... What would she have done? She wasn't sure.

"I'm not sure I agree with you, but...." He laughed. "Whether it's good or not, now you know."

"Yes." She settled back on her pillows.

"But, now that I'm calmer, I've reconsidered my advice." His smile dissolved. He stared into her eyes. "I don't think you should marry Ede."

"Oh?"

After her talk with Ede this afternoon, she knew Ede wouldn't marry her. But she wanted to hear of Ede. She hungered for news of him.

Miklos held her gaze. "You should not marry Ede."

"Why not?"

Apparently Ede had not talked to Miklos, not since she had told him she didn't want to marry. Where was Ede? What was he doing? Was he all right?

She cleared her throat, trying not to cry.

Miklos' eyes wandered to the window.

"He has strange ideas. About Hungary. About society."

Ella knew what Ede's ideas were, but she wasn't sure that these were what worried Miklos. And she wanted to hear more about Ede.

"What kind of ideas?"

Miklos refocused on his sister. "He thinks society should change. He thinks we should have universal suffrage, that all

208

adults should be allowed to vote."

She didn't see why everyone shouldn't be allowed to vote. In particular she thought women should be allowed to vote. Ede was right. Sweet Ede was right.

"Is that bad?"

"Yes. It's bad." Miklos shrugged, his palms turned upward. "How can ignorant people, people who can't read, be able to make good choices?"

She thought to herself, maybe we should teach them to read. But she didn't want to argue with Miklos.

"I see your point."

"And do you know why he wants to live in Budapest?"

She knew, but she didn't want to end this conversation. It was, somehow, a tie to Ede and she didn't want to let go.

"Why?"

"He wants to work toward this, what he calls, this new, modern, Western Hungary."

Of course he did. "Is that bad?"

"I think so. I think it will tear apart our good Hungary. We are doing well, ever since the Austrians made us their partners. We are growing and prospering. We have built railroads and factories and people have more money, are living better."

She could not argue with her brother because she didn't know these things. Ede could. What would Ede say? She nodded.

"And Ede." He stood and walked to the window. Turning back to her, he said, "Ede doesn't want to be a lawyer. Did you know that he will not practice law?"

They had talked about it. But now it didn't matter. Ede would go his way and she would... she would find a way to Vienna.

"He wants to spend full time on this...." Miklos shook his

head. "I'm not sure what he would call it. I call it nonsense."

He paced to the bed and back to the window, his hands deep in his pockets. He shrugged.

"He was more reasonable before he went abroad to study."

"But Miklos, you went to Germany to study too."

He stared at her, apparently considering this.

"Yes. Yes, I did. But I studied something real. Engineering. Something useful." He shook his head and shrugged. "But Ede. He studied sociology."

He approached her bed. "Do you know what sociology is?"

She shook her head. In truth, she didn't know.

"It's a made up subject. Not a science. Some new field where people pretend they can understand society. They call it science. They think they can not only understand it, but remake it."

Maybe understanding society was more important than science. "Is it bad to make society better?"

"I suppose, if they knew what they were doing, it would be fine." Miklos exhaled. "But I don't think they know what they're doing, Ella. I think it will lead to bad things."

Ella remembered her talks with Ede. What he wanted couldn't be harmful. "Bad things?"

"Yes. What these sociologists plan to do will lead to unrest. It will be unsafe."

Ella swallowed.

"Anyhow." He smiled, but his eyes were soft and sad. "I plan to go home tomorrow." He sat on the bed again. "I think you should come with me."

Ella thought about home. She would never go home to grim Mother and all the rules. She could not do that. Now that she had tasted this Budapest life, where women could be educated and work and even choose their beaus. She would never go back to that life where women were... something less than men.

But she doubted that she could explain this to Miklos. Ede would understand.

Oh, she had broken with the only person who would understand. She closed her eyes and inhaled, willing her voice to be calm. "I don't think...."

"I know. Mother is hard. But she has been shocked. I think she'll be kinder to you now."

Ella nodded, not trusting her voice to be steady, not trusting that she would not cry.

"And going to a convent might be a good place. You enjoy books. Maybe we can find a place for you at a school."

She had to smile. She needed no convent. She had found something better here in Budapest.

"Or, if you want, I think we can still find a husband for you. A good husband. A good Hungarian husband."

She shook her head.

Miklos, as kind as he was trying to be, didn't understand her at all. She might try to explain, but she was too tired. Too tired to explain or to fight with him. Better to save her strength for what was important, finding work.

"And you will be safe."

Safe, but not the person she wanted to be, the person she knew she could be.

"So what do you think?"

She shook her head.

"Or maybe you could just live at home. Help Mother. Goodness knows Father can afford for you to stay at home."

"Miklos, I don't...." She looked at him. "I think I will stay in Budapest."

He sighed. "OK." His brow furrowed as he compressed his lips. "I could stay here another day, if you want to think about it."

"Thank you for...." She thought how much he had changed since Therese had died. "Thank you for caring so much for me. Thank you. But I'll stay here."

He nodded and walked to the door. "I'll be gone by the time you wake again."

He walked through the door, but then turned to face her again.

"Good luck, Sister."

Getting Better

Ella heard Aunt Ilona's voice. "Is she awake?"

"I don't think so." That was Flora's voice. "But her fever is gone."

"Really?" Ella felt a hand on her forehead. "You're right!"

Ella opened her eyes and looked into Aunt Ilona's brimming eyes. "Oh, my dear girl. We thought we would lose you!"

"Lose me?"

Aunt Ilona picked up her ear horn and turned it toward Ella. "Lose me?"

"Yes, yes. You've been in and out for the last several days."

Ella tried to put together her situation. She looked around the room, the furniture simpler than her mother's, the walls a cream. She was at Aunt Ilona's.

"What day is it Aunt?"

"Friday, my dear."

Ella was glad to see aunt's ear horn pointed toward her.

"What was wrong with me?"

"We think the doctor might have given you too much morphine." Her aunt sighed. "These doctors. Sometimes you don't know if they do more harm than good."

"Morphine?"

"For the pain, Ella. The detective dislocated your shoulder. The doctor said some tissue must have been damaged too since you were in pain even after he relocated the shoulder."

The detective.

Ella remembered the thug!

She remembered Miklos' rant and his recant.

She remembered Ede's dark face and the slammed door.

"Oh." She gulped.

"You were running a fever. Maybe it was not the morphine. Maybe it was flu." Aunt Ilona went to the table and started placing things on a lap tray.

"But you seem better now." She brought the tray to the bed.

"Maybe you will have something to eat?"

"Yes. Thank you."

Ella remembered the slammed door. She had told Ede she didn't want to marry. She didn't want to marry because... she remembered Tante Cecile and Rózsa.

Oh! She must see them.

"My dear girl, you must eat!" Her aunt's voice was more commanding than she had ever heard before.

Ella looked at the tray on her lap and took a bite of bread.

"And Ede!"

Aunt's angry tone startled Ella. She thought of Aunt Ilona, unlike her mother, as someone who was always sweet.

"Ede has not been here to look after you!" She snorted. "Is that the way to treat your bride?"

"Aunt, we will not marry."

"Eh?" The silver horn now faced Ella.

"We will not marry."

"Oh?"

Ella didn't know how to explain this. Even if her aunt could hear, Ella could not explain. She slowly shook her head as she stared at her aunt.

"Oh."

Aunt Ilona's eyes filled and she dabbed them with her handkerchief.

"Maybe it was not the morphine or the flu. Maybe it was a

broken heart?"

Ella wanted to hug her. "Maybe."

She nibbled her food.

Ede.

She must not think of Ede.

She must figure out what to do.

She must see Tante Cecile.

Rózsa would be furious, impossible. She would say Ella was unreliable. She did not show up when expected, she did not return materials, and worst of all she had lost the pamphlet.

But maybe Tante Cecile would understand. It was not her fault that she was abducted, though the story of her angry fiancé was embarrassing. But if anyone would understand, Tante Cecile would understand.

Ella wanted to work. Tante Cecile was the obvious route to work, to self-sufficiency.

But how to see her? She could just go to her apartment, but Cecile might not be in. But she would be in for her salon. Saturday was her salon. Tomorrow was Saturday.

"Aunt Ilona?"

Ilona picked up her ear horn and turned it to Ella.

"Aunt Ilona, I must go to a friend's afternoon tomorrow."

Aunt Ilona let the hand holding the ear horn drop to her side.

"Oh, dear girl, I don't think you will be well enough to go out tomorrow." She shook her head. "I think after everything you must rest for a while, for several days."

Ella thought that she would burst if she had to wait for another salon, another whole week, before seeing Tante.

"Oh, I am quite well now."

She rolled her shoulder. It was sore, but not painful. She lifted her arm, trying to conceal a wince.

"See. My arm is fine."

She set the tray of food to one side and slid out of bed. Her stomach churned and the room whirled. She focused on Aunt Ilona.

"See. I'm fine."

Ilona shook her head. "Dear, I would worry about you if you went out."

"I must see this friend. It is most important."

"Does it have something to do with Ede?"

Oh, her sweet aunt, always trying to understand, making up little lies for her.

Ella nodded.

It was almost the truth.

She must find work so she would not be forced to be anyone's wife.

Ilona looked at her a long time. She sighed.

"Very well. But I will send you in a carriage and it will wait for you. If you feel unwell, come straight back!"

Salon

When Ella woke the next morning her gaze wandered around the room. She rolled her shoulder. It was quite comfortable today. She remembered the slammed door and sighed. It was Saturday. She remembered the salon and her conversation with Aunt Ilona.

She was going to that salon.

She slid out of bed, leaning against it. The room spun less than yesterday. She took a step toward the table. She was steady. She took another step and another. She would be all right. She could go to Tante's salon.

"Hello."

Ella looked up to see Flora at the door.

"Breakfast?"

"Thank you, yes!"

Flora placed the tray on the table. "You're at the table this morning, Miss. You must be feeling better!"

"Yes, yes. Very well."

Flora poured coffee for her.

Aunt Ilona bustled into the room. "Look who is having breakfast at the table this morning!" She sat across from Ella and poured herself a cup of coffee.

"Are you really feeling well enough to go to your friend's this afternoon?"

Ella put on a smile and raised her voice, hoping her aunt could hear. "Yes, indeed."

"Very well." Ilona sipped her coffee. "I've hired Andras to

217

take you." Andras was the coachman Aunt Ilona used. "He will pick you up and wait for you until you are ready to come home."

"Thank you!"

"And I've found some fresh clothes for you."

"Oh, Aunt Ilona, that is so kind!"

"Not beautiful, but they are decent. You will feel better wearing fresh clothes."

Ella stood to hug her aunt. "Thank you!"

How was it that her aunt was so willing to support her and her mother was so determined to mold her? Were they really sisters?

That afternoon, after she had taken a proper bath and swept her hair up in a gentle bun, she looked at herself in the mirror.

She had grown thinner and paler. She was solemn.

She placed the emerald necklace on her blouse, but that felt wrong. She could not show it to the world. She could not even show it to herself. Her breathing quickened, her eyes welled as she touched the emerald's facets and ran her finger along the diamonds. But she had grown accustomed to its weight on her chest. She would feel, not naked, but incomplete, without it. She tucked it under the soft cotton of her blouse.

Andras helped Ella into the coach and took his seat to drive the carriage. Ella leaned back on the cushions looking out at their route, a path she had walked just a little more than a week ago.

She had been on an adventure then.

Now she was on a mission.

She must explain to Tante what had happened, hoping that she would understand. She wanted Tante's help. That was selfish, but it was true. She had made so much progress toward her goal: work and independence. Tante was the foundation of that progress.

She wasn't sure Tante would understand. If she didn't, then Ella would have to start again, maybe by appealing to Rózsa, though she thought Rózsa would be less likely to forgive her. Or maybe Suska, if she could find her.

Those were contingencies. Perhaps they wouldn't be needed.

The carriage crossed the Chain Bridge and traveled south. Looking to the right Ella could see the Buda Hills across the green-brown Danube.

The carriage turned left onto Tante's street, drove past the little park and stopped in front of Tante's building.

Ella climbed the stairs to Tante's apartment, holding the hand rail, stopping several times to calm her breathing. She knocked on the heavy wooden door.

Mihály opened the door, a smile on his face. When he recognized Ella, his eyes widened and his mouth opened without uttering a sound. He shook his head as if to clear his mind.

"Ella! Our lost Ella!"

Ella smiled. "Hello Mihály!"

She was glad it was Mihály greeting her. She could practice her explanation on him, before she tried it on his mother.

"I'm sorry I disappeared."

Not taking his eyes off her, he stood aside to allow her to enter. "But why?"

"Oh, it was not my idea to disappear!" She looked at him, happy to see his intent look. "I was abducted!"

His eyes grew wider still. "Really?"

"Yes, my family hired detectives to find me!"

Ella wasn't sure of the details. Miklos said that "we" hired detectives, but she wasn't sure whether we meant her family or if it included Ede.

"They captured me." She shrugged, happy that she could do it without much pain. "And dislocated my shoulder."

His brown eyes softened. "You would think they could have been more careful!"

She laughed. "I guess I wasn't very cooperative."

He smiled, his eyes a little easier. "No, Lady of Another Sort, I suppose you would not cooperate."

She exhaled, relaxing her clenched teeth. He seemed to understand. "I'm so sorry! I've returned to you just as soon as I could."

"Yes, yes. But you are here now."

He grasped her hand and led her to the salon.

The room was crowded and smoky. People stood or sat, sipped drinks, ate tidbits, puffed on pipes. Tilly passed a tray of little savories. Karl passed a tray of sweets.

Mihály made his way through the room, turning this way and that to avoid bumping people, excusing himself when he was blocked.

Finally they stood before the sofa. Onkel Mihály sat at one end, Tante reclined, her head resting on her husband's shoulder, a cigarette at her lips.

Mihály released Ella's hand and nudged her forward. "Mutti, look who I've found!"

"Ella!" Tante's hand dropped and the cigarette rolled from her fingers. Mihály picked it up and crushed it in the overflowing ashtray.

"Ella, my dear!" Tante sat up. "Ella, we were so worried about you!"

She slid over, making room for Ella. "Come sit next to me."

Ella exhaled and settled on the sofa. "I am so sorry, Tante. So sorry to worry you!"

Mihály's smile broadened. "I need to greet our visitors, Ella.

220

But come talk to me when you're free."

"What happened?" Tante smoothed her dress, then stared at Ella, waiting for an explanation.

"I was trying to return to your house from Rózsa's and I got lost. I must have wandered into a bad neighborhood and a man grabbed me."

"Oh, my dear!" Tante's hand flew to her throat. "I should have sent someone with you. It's my fault!"

"No, no. I had lost the map Mausi had drawn for me. It was my fault. I am so sorry!"

"Never mind. But how did you escape?"

Ella retold her story, Tante listening and asking questions.

"So it was your family who abducted you."

"Yes."

"And are you to be married then?"

"Oh, no!" Ella studied Tante's face, looking for signs of approval. "I want to be on my own. I want to work." Her eyes wandered to the floor. "But, well, I'm afraid Rózsa will think I am terribly unreliable and...."

Tante laughed. "Oh, she'll grumble all right. She's already grumbled." Tante snorted. "But don't worry. I'll take care of her."

The excitement over, Tante withdrew a cigarette from her case.

"But where are you staying?"

"At my Aunt Ilona's, in Buda. She's been terribly kind."

"Wonderful."

Tante lit her cigarette.

"Are you ready to work?" Tante's eyes skimmed Ella's face. "You're looking a little pale."

"Oh, I'm fine."

Ella wasn't sure how fine she was, but she felt she needed to be available and reliable so this opportunity wouldn't slip away.

"I will see Rózsa in the next day or two. We will find work for you."

As she looked at Ella she exhaled her blue smoke.

The pungent fumes irritated Ella's eyes.

"Thank you!"

"By the way, we've met a fellow from Nagykanizsa, Dr. Herczeg. Perhaps you know him?"

Dr. Herczeg? Ella put her hand on the sofa to steady herself and closed her eyes.

That must be Dr. Ede Herczeg. He had his PhD, so people would address him with the title 'Doctor.' She had never heard him called Dr. Herczeg. It was so formal. It placed him at a level far above hers.

"Ella, dear, are you not feeling well?"

Ella, looking at Tante, forced a smile. "I'm fine."

"Yes. Dr. Herczeg is here somewhere." Tante's eyes swept the room and then she waved her cigarette toward the far corner.

Ella's gaze turned in the direction Tante indicated and she saw Ede near the salon door, several people encircling him.

Her throat constricted.

"Ah, you do know him!" Tante said triumphantly. "You should say hello!"

Ella nodded.

"And he was to marry you?"

How could Tante know that?

"Oh, Ella dear, it is written all over your face."

It was as if Tante were reading her mind. It was all too much.

Fatigue swept over her and she felt the room swim. She

would like to scurry away so that Ede would not see her. But Tante would notice. She must pretend it was all under her control. She must act like everything was just the way she wanted it to be.

"Tante, I am a bit tired. I will say hello to Dr. Herczeg and then be on my way."

"Yes, yes, my dear." Tante patted Ella's knee. "You are looking a little worn out. You go and rest. I will be in touch. Does your aunt have a telephone?"

Ella heard Tante bragging about her new-fangled instruments. She gave Aunt Ilona's full name so that Tante could call her.

Ella took a deep breath and approached the group surrounding Ede.

He was talking to Laura.

Tall, slender Laura, her hair up in a fine style, a silk scarf of blues around her collar, her wide eyes, looking at him. Ede's laugh drifted through the smoky room. Laura's dark eyes lit up, with a broad smile on her perfect lips, a delighted look on her face.

Maybe Ede would marry someone like Laura, someone who had gone to university, someone educated, someone who could talk properly about all the things Ella did not understand, things like the bourgeoisie and the proletariat, like universal suffrage and the nationalities.

Laura's eyes drifted to Ella.

"Ella!" She hugged Ella. "What happened to you? You disappeared into thin air."

Ella nodded. "Yes, yes. I met with some adventures." She tried to smile. "I'm a little tired right now, just on my way home. I've told your mother all about it."

"Well, I'm happy you've reemerged. I was concerned."

"Thank you."

Ella was feeling wobbly. She put her hand on Laura's arm to steady herself and looked at Ede.

He looked away.

After Salon

"Ella dear, you really should eat some supper."

Ella opened her eyes. Aunt Ilona looked down on her, her lips puckered with concern. Ella inhaled deeply so she could speak loud enough for her aunt to hear.

"I'm sorry. I must have fallen asleep."

"No wonder, going into Pest for an afternoon after being so ill."

Aunt Ilona smoothed a lock of hair from Ella's forehead.

"You should eat, child. You need to gain your strength back."

Ella sat up. She took in another deep breath and bellowed. "Yes, yes. I will."

"I could have Flora bring supper here, if you're too tired to come to the dining room."

"No. I'm coming. I'm fine now. Really."

The two of them settled at the table in the dining room. It was a lovely room, not large, but inviting, even in the summer gloaming. A lofty oak tree was visible through the large window, the branches swaying in a gentle evening breeze. Flora had not turned on the lamps yet.

"Did you accomplish what you wanted at your friend's this afternoon?"

What interesting words her aunt used. She understood more than she let on. She knew Ella thought it was important to go to the salon. She didn't know why, and being tactful, she didn't ask. Ella wondered again at her aunt's support.

"Yes, thank you. I think I did."

Ella dipped her spoon in the consommé.

"Aunt, might you have a map of Budapest?"

"I must have one."

She turned toward the kitchen's doorway.

"Flora, do we have a map of Budapest?"

Flora appeared, wiping her hands on a towel.

"We do somewhere, Ma'am. Do you need it tonight?"

Flora's mother had worked in Grandmother's house and the young Flora had tagged along with her mother. When Aunt Ilona was married, she brought Flora along with her to be her cook.

By now Flora was more than a cook. She was a member of the family, especially since Ilona's husband had died.

Ella smiled at Flora. "Thank you. I don't need it tonight. When you have time would be fine."

"Very well, Miss." Flora disappeared back into the kitchen.

"Why are you interested in a map of Budapest, child?"

"I must learn my way around, Auntie."

"Learn your way around?"

"Yes, dear Auntie."

Ella wondered how much she should say. If she told Ilona her plans, the news would get back to her parents. Maybe that was good. Better to send the information through Ilona then trying to explain herself.

"My dear auntie, since I am not to be married, I will need to find a way to support myself."

Ilona's forehead wrinkled with concern.

"I have found some friends who will help me find work, as a children's tutor."

Ilona inhaled. "Oh, my dear child, that'll not be an easy life."

Ilona was right, it would not be an easy life, but she hoped it would allow her to be her own master. She didn't think Ilona would understand, so she just nodded.

"Surely your parents can find you a husband."

Ella had to smile. Why did the world think that the only proper position for a woman was wife?

"It would be difficult to find a husband for me now, now that the engagement with Ede has been broken."

Ilona nodded.

Everyone understood how a broken engagement tainted a woman. She was found lacking after an initial "taste," something like meat that had gone bad.

Ilona cast her eyes down.

"Cheer up, Auntie. It will be an interesting life. I will learn all kinds of things."

Ilona nodded and smiled, but her sad eyes betrayed her attempt at a better mood.

"And, Auntie, might I stay with you a little longer, until I find a position and can find myself a room?"

"Oh." Auntie must be digesting the idea of Ella living in a room by herself. She patted her lips with her napkin, perhaps to hide her frown. She cleared her throat.

"Of course, my child. You are welcome here. Old widows like company. Maybe you could even stay here once you have a job, to keep your ancient auntie company."

"Thank you!" She pushed up from the table, went to Ilona, hugging her. "I would like that."

Ella excused herself right after supper. She was exhausted. It had been a busy day, a good day, even a successful day. Tante was not upset with her and would still help her find work. She could stay with Aunt Ilona, kind sweet Ilona. Everything was going smoothly. Everyone at Tante's had been so nice. Not just Cecile, but Mihály, and even Laura.

Elegant, beautiful, intelligent Laura, her gaze on Ede. Laura who chose her beaus, her eyes sparkling. And Ede, his smile turned to her, favoring her with his mellow laugh.

Ella swallowed.

Her eyes welled.

She pushed her face into the pillow to smother her sobs.

Work!

Ella climbed the stairs to Rózsa's office, Flora a few steps behind her. Aunt Ilona hired Andras to take her to Pest again and didn't insist, but wanted Flora to accompany her.

Ella wasn't sure why this trip seemed to require a companion, while the journey to the salon did not, but she didn't argue. The main object was to get to Rózsa's.

She wondered how she might manage if she had work in Pest. How would she get back and forth? She couldn't afford to hire Andras for every trip, not on a tutor's wages.

She had asked Flora about using the tram that ran between Buda and Pest. Flora had been discouraging. The trams were very crowded, slow, and used by drunks, rag men, and similar unsavory characters.

Another problem to be solved.

But she shouldn't borrow trouble. She didn't have work yet. She would figure out transport when she knew where she had to go.

She knocked at Rózsa's door.

Rózsa glared as she opened the door, her glasses seeming to enlarge her eyes. "I expect you to replace the pamphlet you lost!"

Ella stepped back, bumping into Flora.

"Oh!" She gulped, remembering Tante's warnings about Rózsa: don't argue.

"Yes, of course, I will replace it."

She wasn't sure how to get a replacement or how much it

would cost.

Not having found a fight, Rózsa quieted, her voice an octave lower.

"Well, then, come in. We have business to discuss."

Ella entered the room, already crowded with others. Flora hesitated at the door.

"I'll wait in the carriage, Miss." She retreated.

It was only then that Ella looked around the room, seeing Tante. She nodded at Tante.

And Ede!

Why was Ede here?

"Hello, Ella!" Tante grinned. "I understand you and Dr. Herczeg have met before."

"Yes."

Ella looked at Ede. His brows lifted and then settled darkly in a grimace. He must have been as surprised at this meeting as she was. He studied the floor.

Tante's eyes darted between the two young people.

"Dr. Herczeg was interested in meeting Rózsa, and since I was coming to see her today, I invited him along."

Ella was sure Tante had not invited Ede today as a convenience. She knew exactly what she was doing.

Tante focused on Rózsa. "Rózsa, Suska told me about a book that she thought should be translated, a book in your library."

"Which book is that?"

Tante rubbed her chin. "Oh, I can't remember the title. Something about marriage."

Rózsa snorted. "That would include about half my books."

"Yes, of course. I could probably remember the name if I saw it."

Tante headed to the other room, where most of the books were kept.

"Come Rózsa, help me find it."

Rózsa frowned, sighed, and followed Tante.

Ella looked at Ede, who had taken one of the two chairs in the room, his eyes on his folded hands.

"Ede."

She didn't know what she wanted to say.

"I want to still be your friend."

His eyes still cast down, he exhaled a nasty little snort.

"We have always been friends."

Silence.

"Always."

He cleared his throat, but his voice was gruff when he whispered.

"We were friends when I understood you."

"Understood me?"

He looked up at her, his face white, his eyes hard.

"I thought I did. I thought I understood your hesitation when we talked about having children. I thought I understood when you wanted to know about contraception. But now."

His body lurched in a silent mirthless laugh.

"Now, you just don't want to be married."

He bobbed his head.

"No reason. You just don't want to be married."

Ella bit down on her lower lip. She had her reason. But she couldn't tell him.

"Maybe you don't want to be married to me in particular. If so, I must be detestable." He exhaled, his shoulders sagging.

"Or maybe you just don't want to marry at all." He shook his head. "Which I don't understand." He lowered his eyes.

"I suppose I have a choice: to think myself undesirable or to not understand you. I choose to not understand you."

Ella's tried to inhale, but her throat had tightened and she could not breathe. Of course he didn't understand, because she hadn't told him the reason.

"There is something...."

Tante's gleeful voice rang out from the other room. "That's it."

Ella didn't want to marry, but she hadn't thought she would lose Ede's friendship. She had to explain.

"There is something else, some other reason...."

How could she possibly tell him?

Tante entered the room, holding a large volume. "*'The History of Human Marriage'*. Suska said this was an important book, one that needed to be translated."

Ede stood up and held out his hand for the book.

"May I?"

Tante gave it to him. He sat again, paging through the table of contents. He nodded.

"Yes, yes." He looked up at Tante. "An important book. I should have thought of this as an important project."

He looked down and turned the page. "You said Suska recommended this?"

"Yes, yes." Tante's broad smile betrayed her triumph. "Suska Agoston."

"I should like to be introduced, Tante."

"Of course, Dr. Herczeg." She gave him a quick nod. "So you think this is a book that should be translated? A project you would support."

"Yes, indeed."

"Then I propose that you hire Ella to do that translation."

Ella gaped at Tante. Not only had this meeting been engineered by Tante, so had the assignment.

"Just a moment." Rózsa's shrill voice interrupted. "I have found several tutoring positions for Ella." She puckered her lips. "At your request, if you don't mind."

Rózsa's face grew red. Ella thought she would explode into a rage.

"She will take those positions. Otherwise I will ignore your future requests."

"Now, now, Rózsa, my dear." Tante gave her a little smile. "I am sure that Ella can handle the positions you have found and also work on this translation."

Ella looked from one conniving woman to the other. She wanted work. She was happy to have the tutoring jobs. And she wanted to have a chance to win Ede's friendship back.

"I will be able to handle the tutoring and the translation."

"Of course you can." Tante looked from Ella, to Rózsa, who seemed a little less agitated, to Ede, who leaned back in his chair, his eyes closed.

"Then it's settled."

Ella Explains

Aunt Ilona's offer of room and board came with requirements. They weren't spoken requirements, but they became obvious one after the other.

Ella needed to behave like a proper lady, and proper ladies didn't walk on the streets of Buda by themselves. The tutoring job that Rózsa had found was, fortunately, in Buda, an easy stroll from Ilona's, but Ella's aunt insisted that Flora walk her to the tutoring appointments and pick her up once the session was complete.

Ella supposed she could object, but she had sympathy for her aunt. Her aunt was such a good-hearted woman and she was doing what she thought was proper. But it was more than that. She was doing what the neighbors thought proper. Ella needed to honor that.

Similarly Aunt Ilona insisted that Ella was not to meet a single man in his hotel room. Ede would come to dinner or tea and, after he had been properly fed, the two young people could work.

So it was that a week after the meeting at Rózsa's, Ede entered Ilona's salon. He embraced Ilona, kissing her on each cheek and presenting her with a bouquet of summer flowers.

Ella stood behind Ilona, apparently unnoticed.

"Oh, Ede, such pretty flowers!" Ilona smiled broadly. "I'll just get a vase for them."

She rushed from the room, leaving Ede standing, straight and stiff.

"Hello, Ede." Ella tried to smile, but the angry-school-teacher look on Ede's face made it hard. "Won't you sit down?"

He nodded and sat on one of the overstuffed chairs. He opened his brief case and pulled a large book from it.

"I thought you might find this helpful."

Ella took the book, recognizing Ede's Hungarian-English dictionary, the one she had longed for when she was translating *The Fruits of Philosophy*.

"Thank you!"

She looked at his still stern face.

She couldn't blame him.

This was not his idea.

She supposed he had accepted Tante's proposal just so he would not seem churlish, to stay in Tante's good graces.

"I do have a list of words I didn't know. I will just look them up now and you can take it back with you."

It was a good excuse to retreat from Ede's irate presence.

Ella ran into Aunt Ilona at the door.

"Where are you going, dear? Dinner is ready."

They settled at the table. Flora had prepared a splendid meal, a light consommé to start, roast pork with cucumber salad and new potatoes, and fruit and Brie for dessert.

Ede talked to Ilona, asking her about her childhood on the farm near Zalasárszeg, about her life in Budapest, about her late husband, Sandor, who had owned a flour mill with his brother.

Ilona chatted, looking at Ella now and again.

Ella kept her eyes down, pushing the meat around her plate.

"Well, my dears, you should work in Sandor's office."

She ushered them down the hall to the room past the salon.

"Flora has taken the covers off and freshened it."

She opened the door.

"It is nice to have this room used again."

Ella stepped into the office. Sandor's desk faced the door, a painting of a young, beautiful Ilona over it. Two substantial chairs covered in a dark fabric faced the desk, with a little table between them. A window looked out on the villa's private garden. Across from the window, a sofa, matching the chairs, stood pushed against the wall.

The room smelled of furniture polish and floor wax, but the opened window brightened the space and let in a soft summer breeze.

"Come, Ede." Ilona beckoned to Ede.

He entered and took one of the chairs.

"Well, children, work hard." She smiled at them, as she backed out of the room. "While you labor, I shall take my afternoon nap."

"I've got to get my things." The book and her translation were in her room. "I shall be right back."

As she left the office she exhaled. She could hardly believe this angry Ede had been her friend. Maybe this distant Ede was better. She would translate the book. She would earn her money. And on the basis of that work she might get more work, more translations.

It would be fine.

When she returned, Ede was gazing out the window.

Ella put on a false smile. "While you review the translation, I'll look up the questionable words."

"Very well."

Ede sat, taking the translation from her and a pen from his pocket. He started reading.

Ella placed her list of words on the desk and sat. After each word she found, she would glance up at Ede.

His face was relaxed now, the stiffness of his body smoothed away. He would make a note on the page, then continue reading.

When Ella had come to the end of her list of problem words, she folded her hands, waiting for Ede to finish.

He looked up, a little smile on his face.

"This is good, Ella. Very good." He pointed to the chair next to his. "Come, sit and let's talk about it."

She did as he had asked.

"This word, 'ethnography', you have translated as 'sociology'." I think it is a little different."

She nodded.

"Of course, these are words you have not run into before."

She smiled. "And your dictionary hasn't either! It was the first word on my list, and it's not in your dictionary."

The sound of his laugh, the beautiful melody of his laugh sang out, piercing her heart, choking her lungs, closing her throat.

She coughed.

She looked away, but she could not stop the tears.

Or the sobs.

She surrendered to them, letting her body shake with each wail.

"Ella, Ella." Ede knelt before her holding her shoulders. "What is it, Ella?"

"There is a reason."

She tried to draw in a breath, but sputtered. Closing her eyes, she willed herself to be calm.

"There is a reason I left."

He wiped her eyes with his handkerchief.

"All right." He looked deep into her eyes.

She inhaled, shuddering. "But I can't tell you."

"You must tell me. I need to understand. I need to

understand you."

"But Ede, this is...." She swallowed. "This is...."

"Ella, I know it can be hard to explain." His eyes swept across her face. "I remember how hard it was to tell you...."

"I remember."

She shook her head. She remembered his confession. But she had not demanded it. He had confessed because he wanted to.

"This is different."

Now he was demanding a reckoning.

"This is harder."

"OK. It's harder." Impatience clipped his words. "But I need to know."

She exhaled. "Do you believe...."

She looked past him, her hand grasping the chair's arms so her fingers grew numb. "

"Do you believe Father is a good man?"

She looked at him, waiting for the answer.

His hazel eyes held her gaze.

"Uncle has always been kind to me."

"And Mother? Have you ever known her to lie?"

"Auntie can be quite stern and demanding, but I have never known her to lie."

He returned to his chair, resting his elbows on his knees and his chin on his hands.

"But, what does this have to do with your leaving?"

"Everything."

He stared at her not saying a word, not moving. Just waiting.

The wall clock ticked. "Mother said...."

Ella gulped.

"Yes?" Ede sat up, his eyes on hers, insistent.

"Mother said that...."

238

Ella shook her head.

"I don't know how to say this...."

She closed her eyes, so she felt as if she were not telling him, making it easier to let the words flow.

"She said that Father did disgusting things, that he made her do disgusting things, that...."

She opened her eyes and returned his stare.

"She said that if she did not do these things... he would... he did... he hurt her."

She gulped again, her eyes welling.

"She said that men are bigger and stronger than women–" How could she say these things to Ede, accusing him of.... "–and that if we did not obey them, they would hurt us."

Ede shook his head no, but she continued.

"I told her you would never do that to me, and she laughed at me."

Ella's voice was a raspy whisper.

"Ah, yes, she said, that was what I thought. Everyone thought, she said, that Father was a kind, generous man, a good man, but on the wedding night...."

"Ella, my beloved Ella...."

She interrupted again. "Miklos said I will have to obey you if we were married."

"Yes, my dear, dear Ella. I understand."

She waited for him to deny that it would be like this. He stood, facing the window, so Ella saw his profile, his forefinger tapping his lips. Finally, as if he had made a decision, he turned to her and stroked her head. "Thank you for telling me. Truth is your greatest gift."

She waited for more. For a denial. For something. But there was nothing, though his eyes were no longer stern. They were thoughtful. Ella knew that look, when Ede was thinking, forming a plan.

She studied him. She did not get the denial she wanted. She could not demand it. She searched his face. The denial wasn't there.

She sighed. She probably would never get it. But that was all right. She had explained herself and she thought he understood.

He understood and he was her friend again.

Clara Comes to Town

The sun, filtered by the oak tree, shone into the dining room as Aunt Ilona and Ella ate their breakfast.

"Clara arrives this afternoon."

Ella looked up from her food. "Clara?"

"Yes." Aunt Ilona smiled as she exhaled. "As you might imagine, your mother has been quite upset, so she has gone to your grandmother's."

She sipped her coffee.

"A good idea, I think."

Kind Ilona, Ella thought. She did not blame Ella for her mother's upset, though it really was her fault. "Of course."

"Clara's been a little lost, without you or her mother, and with your father and Miklos busy at the factory, so your father asked me whether Clara might stay with me for a while."

"That's good."

Ella felt a little numb, but it was good. Clara would be good company. Maybe Clara could even be her "companion," so that Flora would not have to escort Ella to her tutoring job.

"That's very good."

"I thought you would like it. Flora has prepared one of the rooms upstairs. One we haven't used since...." Ilona looked out the window. "Since I can't remember."

She looked back at Ella. "It's very nice really, very nice for a lonely widow, to have a full house."

Ella took a bite of her roll and nodded.

"Of course her tutor is coming too. Moni, is it?"

"Yes."

Ella thought of the middle-aged lady who took care of Clara. One day she might be just like Moni, something between a teacher, a nanny, and a companion for a young girl. It was not such a bad life.

"I think you will like Moni."

"They're arriving this afternoon. Andras will pick them up and I shall go too. Would you like to come?"

Ella would tutor the little Meier boys this morning, but she was free this afternoon.

"Yes, of course."

That afternoon, Ella spotted Clara in the crowd walking toward the terminal, tugging on Moni's arm. When Clara saw Ella she broke free from Moni's grasp and ran to Ella, hugging her, tears running down her face. As she held onto Ella, she whispered questions.

"Mimi, why did you leave? Why aren't you getting married? When are you coming home? It's so lonely without you!"

Ella knelt down, wiping Clara's tears away. "It's OK, little sleuth. We're together now."

She drew the crying child into an embrace. Ella blinked away tears. She had not considered how her actions affected Clara.

Clara's sobs subsided and Ella held her at arm's length. "I am so happy you are here." Then she whispered in Clara's ear, "Be a brave soldier. Put a smile on your face. Say hello to Aunt Ilona."

Clara did smile and turned to her aunt. "Hello, Aunt Ilona."

Aunt Ilona ruffled Clara's hair and pulled her ear. "So glad you came, Clara. We shall have a splendid time here. We have all of Budapest to explore."

"What would we explore?"

Ella thought Aunt Ilona should have been a mother. She wondered why Ilona never had children.

"Well, here in Budapest there are some lions that don't have tongues."

Clara's eyes grew wide.

Reviewing the Galley Proofs

Clara wasn't the only surprise that day. Aunt Ilona had invited Ede for supper. Or, to be precise, Ede had telephoned to say he had some things he wanted Ella to work on and might he stop by in the early evening, so Aunt Ilona had suggested he join them for supper.

Ella was nervous. Clara might question Ede about the broken engagement, so she tried to explain as they walked near Aunt Ilona's house.

"But why not marry Ede?"

"Perhaps I am someone who is not... just not meant to be married."

"You mean you want to become a nun?"

Ella snorted. "No." She was directing their steps to Castle Hill. "I don't think I would make a good nun."

Clara looked up at her sister and nodded solemnly. "Probably not."

It was so nice to have Clara here.

"But why not marry?"

Ella chuckled mirthlessly. She had told Clara about sex, but she could not tell her what Mother had said.

"I just would like to be on my own. Make my own way in the world."

"Oh." Clara walked in silence, perhaps digesting this idea. "Well, I want to marry."

"Most ladies marry."

Ella wasn't sure they ever considered anything but marriage.

"If you don't marry Ede, I want to marry Ede."

Ella inhaled. "You are a little young to be considering marriage, don't you think?"

"Maybe." Clara's serious eyes held Ella's gaze. "But Ede is a member of our family and if you don't marry him, then I must."

They had reached the gate to Corvin Hall at the Buda Castle. "Isn't this nice?" Ella pointed to the top of the gate, maybe five meters off the ground. A black iron raven stood there, a ring in his beak.

"That looks like the raven on King Corvinus's coat of arms."

Ella nodded. "I hadn't thought of that before, little sleuth, but I think you're right."

When Ede entered the salon that evening, Clara ran to him, hugging him. He bent down, pulling her to him and she whispered in his ear. Ella wondered if she was proposing marriage, because his mellow laugh filled the room.

"We'll see, Clara. We will see."

Ede set his brief case down and kissed Ilona on both cheeks. He held Ella at arm's length, his hazel eyes searching hers.

"Ella, my dear."

He kissed her on both cheeks too, a chaste familiar greeting.

He nodded at Moni and inquired about the journey from Nagykanizsa.

After the simple supper, Aunt Ilona took Clara by the hand.

"I've got a book all about Budapest. We should look at it while Moni unpacks." She led the child and Moni out of the dining room.

Ede stood. "I've some things I need to discuss with you, Ella. Let's go to Sandor's office."

Ella wondered what they had to discuss, but she was happy just to be with him. "Of course."

Ede called out to Flora. "Might you bring us a little wine,

Flora? To the office?"

This was curious, strange that he would make such a request, as if he were in his own house. But Ella did not object.

Once he had poured Ella some wine and took some himself, Ede sat on the sofa and rummaged in his briefcase. He pulled out a thick stack of paper.

"These, my dear Ella, are the galley proofs for my book."

"Your book?"

"Yes. My book *'Women of Tomorrow'*."

He smiled at her.

"They are proofs that need to be read. All the errors need to be weeded out." He sipped his wine. "And I don't have time to do it."

Ella folded her hands in her lap so they wouldn't reach for the pages. She yearned to read what he had written.

"I thought that getting this done, right now, is more important than translating the other book." He studied her. "I hoped you might be willing to read these proofs for me."

"Yes, of course." She was sure he could sense her excitement, how much she wanted to read the book. "What's it about?"

"It is about my crusade." He flipped through the pages and then looked up. "I think you will like it."

She was quite sure she would.

"But it needs to be done in two weeks. Do you think you can finish in that time?"

"I don't know. I've never done anything like this before...."

"Yes, of course." He cupped his chin in his hand. "Why don't you look at it tomorrow and I will stop by in the evening. You can tell me whether you think you can do it then."

"That's fine."

"Who knows? Maybe I can even get another free supper from Aunt Ilona."

She looked at him, at the sweet smile on his lips, at his soft eyes. His humor had returned. She felt the tension in her shoulders fade.

He lifted his glass. "To our book."

She wondered at this. It was his book.

Reaching his glass toward her, he said, "Prost!"

She leaned forward and they touched glasses. He took a hearty swallow. She watched him and then sipped her wine. She liked this renewed friendship. She settled in her chair comfortably.

His eyes slowly swept over her face. "You look charming tonight."

He cleared his throat.

"I have something else I want to discuss. I want to talk about...." His eyes met hers and he held her gaze. "About difficult topics."

She nodded.

He looked past her, avoiding her eyes.

"About what your mother told you."

She set her glass on the table. She needed a clear mind.

He swirled the wine in his glass and stared at the translucent rose liquid. He looked up at her.

"I considered seducing you, but...."

She sat up straight, her heart pounding.

Ede's smile was soft. "Not rape, my Kis Maria. Seduce."

She nodded and bit her lower lip.

"I even came prepared."

He pulled a small packet from his pocket.

"So we would not conceive a baby."

She stared at the packet, wanting to hold it, to understand how it was used, but what Ede had to say was more important.

"I decided against seduction."

He drained his glass and poured himself more wine.

"Seduce, from Latin, se, away and ducere, to lead. To lead away. To lead away from your duty. Something like that. Not a good way to begin a love life."

Begin a love life? Was this the real reason for his coming tonight, not the book, but this?

She lifted her glass taking a good swallow.

"I don't see why we should not believe what your mother told you."

Ella had tried to make sense of it. "Do you think she is crazy? I don't think she would lie, but maybe she imagined the things she told me...."

He frowned. "No. I think Auntie is sane. I believe what she told you. But even if it were not true, we need to talk about it, since it has you so upset." He sighed. "It's hard. Uncle does not seem...." He shrugged. "Cruel or...."

"No."

"But there is something about lust...."

She stared at him. Was he confirming what mother had said, that all men were like that?

"Ella...." He held her gaze. "We are animals...."

His mouth spread in a wry smile. "I don't mean to denigrate animals."

He shook his head. "No, what I mean is that we have instincts and desires."

Ella swallowed. "So every man would be like that?"

"No." He shook his head vigorously. "That is not what I mean at all."

At least this was a denial.

"It's just that if you first admit that we have these desires, this lust for sex, then you can manage it, make it...." Again his hazel eyes held hers. "Make it an honest thing, a sacred thing."

She drew in a breath. "Sacred?"

A smile flickered across his lips. "I know. I don't use that word often. But I do mean a sacred thing."

He drank again.

"And maybe...."

He swirled the wine.

"Well, you can never tell what another person is thinking, but maybe...." He looked up at her. "Maybe, if you don't admit that you are not in control, then maybe it's easier to pretend you are in control, by controlling your wife."

None of this made sense to Ella. "I don't understand."

"No." He nodded, a curious half smile on his lips. "I guess I should not even talk about that. I only know about me. I have desires. I have lust. I would very much like to make love to you."

He looked up at her, his lips pursed together. He quickly looked at his wine again.

"This lust makes me vulnerable." Pink glowed on his cheeks. "I want to allow myself the full pleasure of my lust before you. I want to lay myself naked before you. Naked without clothes? Maybe. But certainly allowing you to see my naked desire. Allowing you to see me at that moment...."

Again he looked up, his face red. Again his focus returned to his glass.

"That will be – if we ever make love – something sacred and true. To allow you to see me at that moment of pure pleasure."

She didn't understand. "I see."

Again he drank.

"But it will not be complete. It will not be true unless you too are vulnerable, so that you have your pleasure and you allow me to see your pleasure. So that we share our vulnerability. So together we surrender...." He looked at her again, his eyes shone. "To our animal lust."

He set his glass on the table.

"That moment of sharing will be sacred."

She could not imagine it.

"But that will happen only when you are ready."

He ran his finger along the lip of the glass.

"Or maybe never."

He slid his hand along his thigh. "I just had to try to explain. I don't know that...." He smiled at her, then sighed and shrugged, apparently shaking off this delicate topic, trying to find something easier.

"So now, if you like, I brought you a book of German poems."

"Love poems?"

"Hmm...." he pulled a slender volume from his pocket and flipped through the pages. "I think there may be one...." Running his finger down a page so the book was fully opened, he read:

> *A gloomy donkey, tir'd of life*
> *One day addressed his wedded wife:*
>
> *I am so dumb, you are so dumb,*
> *Let's go and die together, come!*
>
> *But as befalls, time and again,*
> *They lived on happily, the twain.*

She laughed. "That's a love poem?"

"Yes." His smile was brighter now. "I am sure it is."

"Not exactly *'Let him kiss me with the kisses of his mouth: for thy love is better than wine.'*"

250

"The *Song of Songs* is not a love poem. It's a lust poem." His chin was tucked, his lips held down in a frown, which Ella knew was fake. "Not, as I said a while ago, that I have anything against lust."

She would have liked to touch him.

"Do you really think that love and lust are separate?"

"Of course. It's only our society that wants us to believe they are the same thing, so we can somehow pretend that our animal instincts, our lusts, do not exist."

"And you think we are just animals?"

"Oh, just." He snorted. "Just is a big word!" His smile was gone. "I don't think we appreciate animals enough. I think we would do well to study them."

"But animals can't talk."

"Are you sure?" His eyes lit up. "Maybe they talk and we just aren't smart enough to understand."

"Perhaps. Let's suppose they can talk. But they haven't invented the steam engine."

Ella felt sure she was right.

"They haven't learned to fly like the Wright brothers."

"Some animals already know how to fly." He shook his head, a grin spreading across his lips.

"Maybe we are different from animals, maybe there is a God. I do not know these things. These things we will never know."

"Really? Never?" She stared at him, putting on as serious a face as she could. "Never is a big word!"

His laugh. His delicious laugh.

"Enough of love and lust, animals and man."

He slid to the side of the sofa.

"Come sit next to me." He patted the sofa. "You have to see these poems to truly enjoy them."

She sat next to him, pulling her legs under her and leaning

her head on his shoulder to see the book better. She inhaled his scent of pine, her body nestled into his, as she had done so often before. Comfort flooded her being.

He turned to a page and read:

The Snail's Monologue

Shall I dwell in my shell?
Shall I not dwell in my shell?
Dwell in shell?
Rather not dwell.
Shall I not dwell
Shall I dwell,
Dwell in shell
Shall I shell,
ShallIshellIshallIshellIshallI...?

(The snail gets so entangled in his thoughts or, rather, the thoughts run away with him so that he must postpone the decision.)

She sighed. What wonderful nonsense.

He looked down at her. "I bet you can't translate that into Hungarian."

She looked up into his smiling eyes. "Csiga for snail."

She was sure she could make something work.

"But that also means helix. There are possibilities there."

"And?"

Oh! The challenge! The mischief in his eyes! His wide smile added fullness to his cheeks, his eyes on her, waiting.

She knew there had to be a better approach. Her tongue savored the Hungarian as she spoke. "Shall I leave my little shell?"

He nodded.

Then the words flowed:

Shall I leave my little shell?

Leave my shell or shall I not?

Open wide

and step outside --

or better hide?

I can't decide

to leave my shell

or shall I not?

"Not bad...."

His lips turned down in his fake frown.

"But the word 'hide'...."

He shook his head, the light in his eyes still gleaming.

"You are implying much more than the original poem. You are telling us the motive for the snail's indecision."

"Which is good!" She huffed. "This way we can empathize with the little fellow."

"Yes, yes."

His body shook with his attempt to contain his laughter.

"But you may have the wrong motive. Maybe he's undecided because it's too warm inside and too cold outside." He chortled. "Or maybe there are fleas inside and escargot-eating Frenchmen outside."

She shook her head, grimacing.

"You could help, you know." Sometimes he was so annoying. "Otherwise you will be outside my shell."

He grinned.

"Oh, never mind." She reached for the book. "Let me see it."

Flipping through the pages, looking for something that

might not be so challenging, she stopped at a page with the poem "Fish's Night Song," which looked like this:

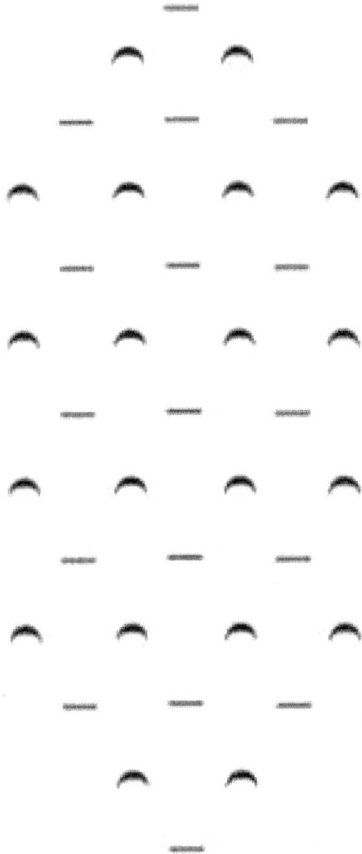

She stared at it, thinking of the possibilities. She showed it to him.

Finding paper, a pen and ink at the desk, she scribbled for a short while, then gave Ede the paper.

"There's your translation!"

His laugh exploded, as he looked at her drawing.

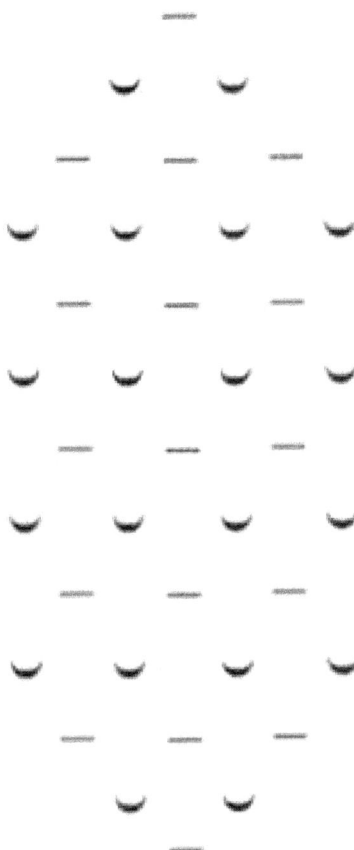

He wiped the tears from his eyes as his laughter subsided.

"Oh, my Ella. My brilliant Ella." He pulled her to him.

She loved him. She put her hands on his cheeks, pressing her lips to his.

His hands were on her face, her neck, her shoulders, on her breasts. He pulled away from her.

"My beautiful Ella!"

He brushed his finger along her cheek.

"I love you beyond words."

He stood and placed the book of poems in his briefcase.

"I must go."

"But why?"

"I don't want to leave." All trace of humor had faded from his face. "But it's best that I go."

And he was gone.

She touched her face, her neck, following the path his fingers had taken.

She trembled.

Women of Tomorrow

The next morning after breakfast, Ella took Ede's book into Sandor's office, sat at the desk, and flipped through the pages.

The first chapter was the essay she had read, so long ago it seemed, *The Sorrows of Sex*.

The next chapter compared men and women. Men, according to one argument in the book, had heavier brains and were therefore more accomplished than women. Ede proceeded to examine the relative brain weight of men of different nationalities.

She laughed out loud when she read that French men's brains, on average, were lighter than German men's brains.

Oh Ede, what a sly one.

Ella read the conclusion of this chapter several times, trying to understand it. It seemed to say women were less intelligent than men. Or was he just saying they had accomplished less?

Intelligence or accomplishment, Ella did not know how one measured these things.

The next chapter discussed possible reasons for the differences between the intellectual capacities of the sexes. Ella read and reread, trying to understand.

Certain comments infuriated her. Could Ede really believe these? Or was he just setting down the argument so he could refute it. She looked out the window, overwhelmed. Finally, knowing she needed to talk to Ede about this, she turned the page to start the next section.

"Mimi?"

Ella looked up to see Clara standing in front of her. She had been so engrossed in Ede's book she had not heard Clara enter.

"Mimi, it's time for dinner."

"Oh, yes." Ella stood. "I'm coming."

Clara grabbed her hand, leading her to the dining room, chattering.

"Auntie is going to take Moni and me to the city park this afternoon."

"Nice."

"She says there are all kinds of wonderful things there, a zoo and a swimming pool, and there's a big surprise at the park."

"Auntie took me there years ago. I think you'll like it."

"Can you come too?"

Ella wanted to read more of Ede's book. It wasn't required, but it was what she wanted.

"Clara, it sounds like so much fun, but I must work today."

Clara stuck out her lower lip and looked down.

"We'll have time for lots of adventures together here. You enjoy the park today. We'll do something special soon. Maybe we could visit Gül Baba's tomb."

"Gül Baba?"

"He was a dervish poet! He was a Muslim, who lived here when the Turks ruled. Sultan Suleiman the Magnificent named him the patron saint of Buda."

"Can he be a saint if he's Muslim?"

Ella had to chuckle.

"I suppose, little sleuth, he was a saint for the Muslims."

The prospect of a dervish poet pleased Clara and during dinner she asked Aunt Ilona about him.

After dinner, Ella returned to the study to read more. She found an index at the back of the book and she used that to read sections she thought she might more readily understand.

258

Ede argued that women should wear sensible clothes. No corsets! Women should eat plenty of fresh vegetables. And get exercise. How could she disagree with that?

He wrote that they should be educated, be allowed to attend classes with boys.

Co-education!

It took her breath away. To be able to go to university seemed beyond her reach. But to be allowed in the same gymnasium as boys? That seemed the foundation for the real opportunity to learn.

Women should be allowed in the professions, just like men. Ella closed her eyes. If she could be anything, what would it be? Her mind swam. So many possibilities.

Women should be allowed to vote. She was startled. She knew nothing about politics. This seemed like a burden to her. She would have a lot to learn before she would vote.

She turned to the last section: *The Responsibilities of Marriage*. It was all there: contraception, abortion and.... Her eyes fell on the sentence:

> *"The law says violent intercourse, rape and infestation with disease are not punishable if the offender and the victim are married before the criminal conviction is pronounced."*

This law, Ede wrote, that allowed men to rape women, to abuse women, whatever their marital status, is criminal.

Ella sighed.

That was the denial she wanted.

And he must have written it before she had asked him about Mother's comments. It was a denial before the accusation, so he must believe it!

Even beyond this, he wrote:

"A woman not only has a legitimate desire for sexual satisfaction. It is required, not only for her health, but for a satisfied and faithful husband, a happy family, and ultimately for the survival of the community at large."

She looked out the window. How could she have doubted Ede? Sweet Ede.

Her eyes wandered back to the book. She turned the page, her eyes skimming here and there, until they stopped on a passage.

Her hand flew to her mouth.

The words, explaining exactly how to stimulate sexual desire in a woman, excited her.

She remembered Ede's touch. She remembered his words: "It will not be true unless... we share our vulnerability and together surrender to our desires."

Book Review

"Ede, you seem a little reserved this evening?" Aunt Ilona stared at him. "Is everything all right?"

He took a sip of his wine. "I'm fine. Just a busy day."

Aunt Ilona was right. Ede had greeted everyone in the usual way this evening, the kissing of cheeks, the ruffling of Clara's head, the polite nod to Moni, but his mind seemed elsewhere.

And during the light evening meal, it was Clara who did most of the talking, about the city park with its animals and the swimming pool, but mostly about the surprise Aunt Ilona had promised: Vajdahunyad Castle, a scale model of several castles that had been important in Hungarian history.

After supper, Aunt Ilona, Clara, and Moni went to Clara's room to read about Gül Baba.

Ella asked Flora to bring some wine to the office.

"Do you think you'll be able to review the proofs?"

The question burst from Ede as he sat on the sofa. Maybe it was what had preoccupied him earlier.

Ella sat next to him. "It is an interesting book."

His gaze skimmed her face as he sat at the edge of the sofa.

She poured wine for him and took some for herself.

"I don't understand some of it."

He nodded. "Of course." The creases on his forehead deepened.

In reality, some of what she read, she just disagreed with, but she hesitated to say more. He, after all, was Dr. Herczeg. She was just Ella. Still she couldn't help herself.

"You say women's inability to compete with men intellectually is caused, in part, by their menstrual cycle."

"Yes. A number of studies show a woman's physical capacity is hindered during her period. And that would hinder her intellectual abilities as well."

Ella knew nothing of the methods of scientific studies, of the literature. Had Cousin Ervin written this book, she might have held her tongue. But Ede wrote it. She trusted he would listen.

"I object on two counts."

"Yes, yes." His eyes, set on her, brightened.

"First, on personal experience. I don't notice my periods. Well, maybe a twinge, but that's all. My period never stopped me from studying, from thinking."

Ede nodded. "Glad to hear this, my dear. But one person's experience is not statistically significant."

Ella considered this. "If I read these proofs, you must teach me statistics, so I will understand."

His eyes shone. "Of course, Ella. We will study statistics."

She was disappointed her objection was so easily dismissed, but she had another.

"You know Ede, it is not just women who have to deal with problems related to their sex." She studied him. "I believe you have spent considerable time worrying about the 'Sorrows of Sex'. How much intellectual work did you get done then?"

"Interesting." He looked off in the distance, slowly rubbing his chin. "We'll have to consider that."

As if he had made a decision his eyes rested on her again.

"You are the perfect colleague, Ella."

She sighed at the 'we'.

"I love most of what I read, about education and careers."

He settled back into the sofa, smiling.

"I am sure I can read it two or three times before the

deadline."

The words came easily now.

"I like your crusade." She shrugged. "At least the parts I agree with."

He chuckled, nodding his head.

"Maybe I want it to be my crusade too."

"Even better." He put down his glass.

"I will read it." She grinned. "But beware, for I am determined to find every single mistake in it."

His eyes were bright, his lips turned down in his fake frown.

"I tremble exceedingly before mine enemy."

She hesitated.

She had pictured what she would do next, but now it seemed forbidding. Did she really want to do this?

Her throat tightened. Her breath came in little wisps.

Yes.

She would do this.

It was what she wanted.

She slid over so their bodies touched. She drew in a deep breath.

"I like what you wrote in the last chapter."

Her fingers trembled as she touched his hair.

"I wish I had read it before you asked me to marry you."

"Yes." His eyes glimmered and grew soft. "It would have been better."

She drew in another breath, willing her voice to be calm.

"But now I understand more."

She leaned her body into his, placing her hands on his cheeks.

"I desire more."

She pulled him toward her, kissing him. She leaned back and looked into his kind hazel eyes.

It was right.

It was what she wanted.

"Let you kiss me with the kisses of your mouth: for your love is better than wine."

She ran her hands along his face.

"Kisses sweeter than poems. Or books. Or crusades."

She saw the glint of tears in his eyes as he drew her to him.

Ella woke, feeling Ede's breath on her face.

"Ella, my own." His fingers brushed her cheek.

She opened her eyes, seeing Ede's sweet smile lit by the full moon filtering in from the window.

"Ella, I must go." He stood reaching for his jacket. "It is quite late and we would not want to..."

She sat up. "Yes, of course."

She smoothed her hair back. "But you must answer one question before you go."

He pulled his jacket on and straightened his tie. "Yes, my beloved Ella, what is it?"

"Will you marry me?"

A Better Way

The next day after dinner, Ella and Ede meandered the grounds surrounding the Buda Castle, Ella stopping at the foot of a statue.

She shielded her eyes as she looked up at the figures of a man and a horse, the horse's head thrown high, his nostrils wide, his haunches flexed, ready to spring free from the man, the man leaning back, putting his full weight into the tug on the bridle's reins, his wide sleeve fallen back, displaying the sinews of his powerful arm. He stares into the beast's wild eye, as if he can convince the animal of his power with his stony look.

"It's magnificent."

"Magnificent?" Ede shook his head. "Moving, yes." He snorted. "But I feel sorry for the beast."

Ella turned her eyes to Ede, considering his words. It was a powerful statue, but sad, sad for the terrified horse.

"Moving." Ede grimaced. "And very Old Hungarian, Eastern, as if man can overcome all adversaries with pure muscle and fierce rage."

Ede put his hand on her elbow and guided her to an overlook of the Danube and Pest.

"Let's look at the view of our new home town."

He rested his hands on the wall surrounding the overlook.

Her eyes ran along the far shore of the river.

"The Parliament building, pure muscle and fierce rage?" She looked at Ede. "Old Hungarian, Eastern?"

He laughed. "It reminds some people of the British

Parliament. Even so, it is very Hungarian and old Hungarian at that. But we will find a way to make it Western."

He looked at her, his smile still broad. "So, my dear fiancée, when do we leave for Nagykanizsa?"

"Nagykanizsa? Why would we go to Nagykanizsa?"

His smile faded, replaced by a quizzical look. "To be married."

"Couldn't we just get married here?"

His forehead creased, his lips frowned. "We might be able to, but it won't be easy."

She pursed her lips. "Why not?"

"Well, among other things, my dear, the state requires the consent of your father, since you are under 20."

She frowned and looked down.

"If you really want to be married here, I think we could get over that hurdle and several others."

She looked up at him smiling. "That is what I want."

His face was serious. "But I wouldn't advise it."

"Why not?"

"To start with, it is cruel to your mother."

"Cruel to Mother?"

"Yes."

He held her gaze, his eyes stern. "All of Nagykanizsa will know that her daughter got married without her father's consent. That she was not married in her hometown."

Ella looked away, but Ede placed his finger on her chin and turned her face to his.

"It will be the scandal she has been trying to avoid. Her friends will shun her."

She felt her cheeks burn. "Mother worries too much about scandal."

"I think you are too hard on your mother. She did what she

266

thought she must to make your life secure."

Ella, looking down, pushed her toe into the wall.

"And Ella." Again Ede's finger on Ella's chin forced her to look into his eyes. "I think it will be hard on your father."

"Father wouldn't care." She shrugged. "He'll probably be happy to be rid of me and my fights with Mother."

She had tried not to think about Father since her mother accused him of such savagery. She didn't know what to think, feeling panicky each time she tried to understand.

"But it may be bad for his business." Ede's lips held a gentle smile. "People may not want to do business with him. How could he keep his business in order if he cannot keep his daughter under control?"

Ella reluctantly nodded.

"But worst of all, it will be bad for Clara."

Ella inhaled and thought of Clara's tears at the train station. She shook her head.

"Her friends will avoid her." Ede stared at her.

"I should care. Especially about Clara, I should care."

She stamped her foot. "But how can I celebrate my marriage to you with my parents, my strange parents, who are mysteries to me?"

She knew she was being childish, but she didn't want anything to do with her parents. She didn't want to think about them.

"Ella, Ella." Ede placed his hand on her arm. "You are being too hard on them."

She shook her head.

"Yes, you are."

His gaze drifted to Pest. He looked back at her.

"Your parents are not bad people. They are good people, trying to do the right thing, but their understanding of 'right' has been twisted by the society that surrounds them.

"Your mother and father are a little like that statue: your mother, like the horse, terrified, just trying to survive; your father, like the man, using his muscles and his anger to do what he thinks he must, control her. They do these things not because they are bad. They do these things because they know no other way."

He smiled.

"And what we want to do, our crusade, is to show the world there is another way. We need to change the system so that people no longer grow up as your parents did. We need to do it for Clara. For all children. For everyone."

He placed his hands on her shoulders and turned her toward him.

"If you make war with your parents, by refusing to follow these marriage conventions, you will convince them of nothing. You will be like the man in that statue."

Ella bit her lip.

"But if you follow these small rules of society, these little rituals, when an important problem arises, one which we cannot foresee, then your parents will be more likely to work with us."

She turned to look back at the statue and thought of Ferenc, who took care of Grandmother's horses. Ferenc had a better way with horses. He was quiet, moved slowly, spoke softly, breathed in their nostrils.

She remembered the day the stallion was put in the corral with the mare. Sure he stomped and snorted, but Ella believed he was full of joy, not terror. And once he noticed the mare, he greeted her and loved her before he mounted her.

What would the horse in the statue do if he were put in a corral with a mare?

She turned to Ede. He was right. There was a better way. The way of Grandmother's horses. The way of last night.

Sweet, sweet last night.

She wanted to touch Ede. To do more than touch him.

She laughed to herself.

Not here. Not in public.

That desire, that was what Ede must mean by lust. But, at least for her, it was more than lust.

It was love.

She smiled at him. "How soon can we leave for Nagykanizsa?"

Before the Crusade

"Well, good afternoon, Miss Weisel." The grin on the station master's face was just as malicious as the day Ella had gone to Budapest alone. "And how is your Aunt?"

"Very well, thank you, Mr. Kovacs." Ella hoped her smile chilled his enthusiasm for gossip. "In fact, there she is."

Ella looked across the railroad station's hall to where Father and Miklos were greeting Aunt Ilona, Ede, Clara, and Moni.

"She's so well that she has come to help with the wedding preparations."

Mr. Kovacs smile remained, but the cynical twinkle in his eye had vanished.

The next day Mother returned from Grandmother's farm. She did not look nearly as well as Aunt Ilona. Her face was pale, her hair dull, her dress hung loosely on her shoulders.

Aunt Ilona put Mother to bed and took charge of the wedding preparations.

Her ear horn in hand, Aunt Ilona visited Father Lajos, who had taken over after Father Joseph's death. She discovered the peasants in Kiskanizsa who could provide beautiful flowers and she worked with Cook to make sure the Kanizsa City Club, where the reception was to be held, had everything for the wedding dinner.

After a week, Mother's complexion was rosier, and she helped Ilona in the preparations. They saw after the invitations, the church flowers, and the dresses for the ladies, the table settings and the table seatings.

But Ilona directed. She directed Ella and Clara, Father and even Mother.

Ella watched Ilona work, amazed that this apparently sweet, old, hard-of-hearing lady could organize the family like a general readying troops for battle.

Finally the wedding day arrived, a late summer day, with a whiff of autumn in the air. Ella's only duty was to dress. While the family buzzed around her, she was happy to sit alone, her soul filled with quiet contentment.

She thought back to the day Ede first proposed they marry. How much had happened! She regretted none of it. Today she knew she wanted to marry Ede. She knew they would make a good life together. She knew they would help make their Hungary a better country. It was that something she had wanted, the inexplicable something she could now explain.

Mother loved the wedding. Ella loved it too. She loved the Czardas dancers and the Viennese orchestra. She loved waltzing with Father, with Miklos, and with Ede's brother.

But most of all she loved dancing with Ede.

Miklos was quiet, spending most of his time talking with Ede's brother. Aunt Ilona fell asleep after the dinner, her silver ear horn on the floor by her hand. Mother talked with her friends, who gathered round chattering. Father went from one table to the next, greeting people, slapping friends on the back, laughing. And Clara danced with every man over thirteen, running back to Ella to boast about her latest conquest.

At last the food had been eaten, the couple had been toasted, the dances had been danced and Ella and Ede, exhausted, boarded the night train for Budapest.

To their new life.

To their crusade.

Please review this book on Amazon.

Author's Notes
Fact and Fiction

This story is based, very loosely, on the lives of my maternal grandparents, Ede Harkányi and Ella Weiser. They were born in Nagykanizsa to wealthy families. Harkányi studied in Switzerland and Germany, earning a law degree and a PhD in sociology. When he returned to Hungary, he moved to Budapest and became active in progressive circles. Being independently wealthy, Harkányi never practiced law, devoting his time to writing and speaking about the rights of women. My grandmother translated *The History of Human Marriage* into Hungarian. This classic book concerned the development of marriage in society. This leads me to believe the real Ella supported her husband's work.

I have a few more crumbs of information about Ella and Ede and their families, but nothing that would answer the riddle: why would a man from a wealthy family leave his home town, go to Budapest, and delve into politics, specifically the politics of women's rights? Hungary, at that time, was a particularly male-chauvinist society, which makes my grandfather's career choices even more mysterious. This novel is my attempt to paint a possible explanation of Harkányi's actions, that he admired his future wife's intelligence and her spunk, and his interest in women's rights grew from her attitudes.

I have invented much of the story. I have made no attempt to research or understand the other members of the Harkányi and Weiser families. What I write about Ella's parents in particular, is pure fabrication, created to make a point. I have therefore changed the family names of my ancestors from Harkányi to Herczeg and from Weiser to Weisel, so there is no doubt that what I have written about them is fiction.

Much of this novel was inspired by Harkányi's book, *A holnap asszonyai* (*Women of Tomorrow*), which was published in 1905. The quotations from it and the essay, *The Sorrows of Sex*, are my translations of his words, with much help from translation programs. Similarly, the summary of sections of the book in the chapter titled Women of Tomorrow is my summation of the contents of his book.

Several characters in the story are historic figures, including Tante Cecile and her family, Rózsa Schwimmer, and Suska Agoston, who will become more important in the next books in this series. The journal, *A huszadik század* (*The Twentieth Century*), was published from 1900 and was the voice of the Hungarian progressive circle, led by Oszkár Jászi, among others. Harkányi and his friends often contributed to the pages of *The Twentieth Century*.

The pamphlet, *Fruits of Philosophy*, was written by Charles Knowlton, M.D., in the mid 1800s. It advocated contraception, which was considered obscene and therefore illegal in the United States and various countries in Europe in the 19th and early 20th centuries.

Acknowledgements

People think writing a book is a solitary endeavor and parts of it are. But I could not have completed this book without the help of a great number of people.

Carol Edge read and commented on the whole book, on its first revision, on the revision to the revision, on the revision to the revision to the revision, ad almost infinitum. She made me see and fill in the dramatic holes. Karen Haas sat with me, tightening up my prose and showing me how to make my language more colorful. Alisa Alering, who first said I should try writing a novel, has helped with all my writing. Comments from Vicki Williams, Judy Shoolery, Jenny Kander, Richard Durisen and Alan Balkema improved the story and the writing.

Writing a historical novel is a challenge because the author must learn the customs, technology, dress, and on and on of a previous time. For this novel I had to cover all those topics and I had to learn about a country I have only briefly visited and a people whose language I do not speak. A number of generous people helped me. Judith Szapor answered many emails and her books on Laura Polanyi Stricker and the Women's Movement pre- and post-World War 1 were immensely helpful. Péter Csunderlik answered questions, sent papers, and suggested additional reading. Janos Kirz not only translated several of my grandfather's papers for me, he read the entire manuscript looking for and finding several cultural blunders. Andrea Peto, Tibor Frank, Peter Czipott, Bill Lanouette, Tamas Bartfai, Drew Senyei, Andras Koerner, and Istvan Hargittai recommended resources to help me understand the Hungarian historical and cultural landscape. Maria M. Kovacs, Ellen Hume, and Jane Landes Foster helped me find all these people.

While writing this book, John Acros, a distant relative, connected with me. John was kind enough to share information about our family and Nagykanizsa.

I am so fortunate to have permission from Anthony Knight and Marty Knight to use their father's wonderful translations of Christian Morgenstern's poems. Howard Stern kindly provided an ingenious additional translation, *Soliloquy of a Snail*, part of which was fictitiously attributed to Ella.

My husband, Richard Weyand, edited the book, designed the book cover, published the book, and listened patiently to all my authorly complaints.

Thank you all!

About the Author

Wendy Teller received her AB from Harvard University and her MA from the University of California, Berkeley. She was a systems and software engineer in the process control and telecommunications industries.

Now that she is retired she writes fiction, memoir, and history. Her stories have appeared in *Chicken Soup for the Soul*, *The Naperville Sun*, and *Rivulets*. Her story *Dusting the Towels* received the Richard Eastman Prose Award. Wendy's debut novel, *Becoming Mia*, takes place in the 1960s in Cambridge, Massachusetts, and Berkeley, California.

Wendy lives on a cliff in the woods near Bloomington, Indiana, with her husband, science-fiction author Richard F. Weyand.

www.ingramcontent.com/pod-product-compliance
Lightning Source LLC
Chambersburg PA
CBHW070318260626
47160CB00003B/882